MY DRAGON KEEPER

Broken Souls 2

ALISA WOODS

Cover by BZN Studio

ISBN: 9781692028022

My Dragon Keeper **(Broken Souls 2)**

When you're destined to be the soul mate of a dragon, what's love got to do with it?

Nothing makes any sense.

I wake up in a hospital bed with no memory of the last two weeks, no idea where I am, and a hot guy tending my every need. Well, not every need… not yet. But he's hot as sin and twice as sweet.

Next thing I know, I'm confessing all my sins—and the darkness I'm still carrying inside.

What have I done that I can't remember?

Then he starts talking about a magical race of dark elves and soul mates and… I'm running for the door.

Because I've finally cracked and none of this can be real.

Cinder's a soft-hearted photographer. Aleks is a

dragon whose time is running out… she might not be his soul mate, but try telling that to his heart.

My Dragon Keeper is a steamy new dragon shifter romance that'll heat up the sheets with love and warm your heart with dragonfire.

ONE

Aleksandr

WATCHING CINDER IS LIKE WAITING FOR A BIRD with a broken wing to heal.

Only I don't know what part of this gorgeous Dragon Spirit has been shattered. Her body is recovering—the dark circles under her eyes are gone; the cracked lips are healed. She's coming back from being starved while captured by the Vardigah, the bastard dark elves who held her and did *something* to her. I'm sure she was taken because of *us*—because she was destined to be a soul mate to a dragon somewhere—and that hangs some fucking heavy guilt on my heart. But that's not why I'm here. And it's not why I haven't left her side for more than a few minutes since we rescued her.

I made her a promise.

Two promises, actually. The first one was out loud for other people to hear. She said something about a girl named Julia, who she wanted me—*us, someone*—to rescue. She said it in one of her fevered states, so I don't even know if that's real... but I promised all the same. The second was a whisper for her alone. That I knew she was Dragon Spirited. That she would live and love and become the mate of some lucky dragon. Even if she hadn't had the mark—the same as her twin sister, Ember, now mated to the Lord of our Lair—I could hear her dragon spirit in her feverish words. Not asking for help. Not crying out for comfort. But seeking help for someone else, someone trapped by an enemy that had waged a genocidal war on my people and nearly destroyed them. *That* was Cinder Dubois' dragon spirit speaking directly to me, and once we were alone, I vowed to that spirit I would not leave her side until she was whole again. Not just the physical recovery from whatever the Vardigah had done, but whatever else she needed, including finding her other half—because that was the very least she deserved for all her suffering because of us.

Cinder makes a small murmuring noise. She shakes her head like she's saying *no*, but then sinks deeper into the pillow. Her beautiful dark hair is fanned out across the white linens. The fever that blushed her pale cheeks for the first few days is gone. It's been two weeks since Cinder returned, and she occasionally wakes and eats, but mostly, she sleeps. Her lips part in a sigh that captivates me. She's talking more now—sometimes when she's awake—but she's still confused. Yet I hang on every word, looking for clues to help her heal. The human doctors can find nothing wrong with her, and dragons don't need medicine—our bodies keep us healthy and youthful in appearance until the bitter end. Once upon a time, we'd give our blood to the witches, and they'd use it for healing spells for humans. I'd give blood for Cinder in a heartbeat, but those arts are lost now.

I'm waiting for her to say something after her sigh, but it doesn't come. She just returns to her light, restless sleep, so I go back to gazing out the window.

We're in the mated dragon's honeymoon cottage, tucked in one of the Thousand Islands, but far from the lair's castle. The cottage is a tiny place, built for privacy, and we're hiding out here in case the Vardigah come back for her. We can't risk them finding the lair and finishing us for good. But Niko-lais—my friend and brother dragon—is on standby to teleport in and rescue her, should the Vardigah come hunting. Ember as well. They're mated, so their powers include that ability among others. I'm standing guard and offering what I hope is comfort during Cinder's recovery. Ember gets freaked during visits, so I think it helps her to know I'm always here.

Not that I would be anywhere else.

Cinder draws in an audible breath and opens her eyes.

I beam a smile and lean forward on my chair next to her bed. "Hello, sunshine."

She squints. "Who're you?"

It spears my chest—I keep hoping she'll remember me from one time to the next. "I'm your friend. Aleks. Are you hungry? Lunch is waiting for you."

She shakes her head, closing her eyes and leaning back into the pillow. I think maybe that's it, but then she sucks in a breath and struggles to sit up. She's still weak, even with the meals we've been able to get into her.

"Where are you going, beautiful?" I'm out of my seat, gripping her arm to help her rise while tapping the controller for the bed to raise the head.

Nikolais ordered one of the hospital beds brought over from the hospice center for the lair.

"Bathroom." She shoos away my help, but I know she's not steady enough to go on her own. Getting close but not yet.

"I'll get the nurse." I tap the call button on the table at her bedside.

"Nurse?" Cinder peers up at me, confused, with those wide gorgeous eyes of hers. They're amber near the pupil, blending with green along the outside, and edged with a dark blue-green that makes them just pop. They're the same eyes that Ember has, but somehow Cinder's are deeper. Or maybe just more broken. The rest of their features are nearly identical—same gorgeous curves, same porcelain skin—except Ember has a tiny birthmark on her cheek. That, and Cinder looks like she's been tortured. They both have the birthmark on the inside of their wrists that shows them as Dragon Spirited.

"Here she comes." I nod toward the door as it swings open, hoping to distract her until the nurse can scurry to her bedside.

"Ah, you are up again!" the nurse trills, hurrying across the room. She's a short Indian woman with a delicate face, surprising strength, and a lovely singing voice, which she's always using. She takes my place at Cinder's side, grasping hold of Cinder's arm to help her up. "Do we need to use the facility?"

"Are you the nurse?" Cinder asks, her brow wrinkling as she stands.

"Yes, dear. I'm Biti, remember? Let's get you taken care of." As the two shuffle-walk toward the restroom, the nurse starts to sing. *"I hope when you decide, kindness will be your guide. Put a little love in your heart…"*

I smile. Biti said something about music being soothing for memory patients, but I think she just likes to break into song. Cinder doesn't have Alzheimers—she's got some kind of amnesia brought on by being attacked by magical creatures. The nursing staff know we have some rare afflictions, but they don't know about the magical side, like the fact that they're serving dragon shifters or that the Vardigah even exist. The nurses simply do what they do best—caring for their patients.

Which gives me a moment to step outside.

I want to be there whenever Cinder awakens—that continuity might eventually put some pieces together—but I grab the chance to get some fresh air when I can. There's a wide balcony off the back of the cottage, and it overlooks a lush garden. Fragrant flowers surround a small fountain, and past that, a wooden lover's swing hangs from a vine-covered pergola. Every dragon in the lair dreams of finding their mate, bringing them here, and christening every inch of the place with their love-making. So far, we've only had six mated pairs—now seven with Niko and Ember, who are honey-mooning at Niko's retreat castle. I breathe in the flower scents and wonder if Cinder would return here with her mate, after she finds him. Would she want to come back to the place where she spent so much time in recovery?

I take the stone steps down from the balcony to the pathway and then past the fountain. The flowers in her room need refreshing, and the daylilies are just opening now that we're moving into mid-summer. I pick a few, linger for a moment to soak in some sun and gaze at the sparkling blue water. When Cinder gets a little stronger, I want to bring her out to the bench swing and let the beauty of the garden banish some of the darkness that seems to plague her. I can't decide if the amnesia is damage the Vardigah did or if it's protection her mind has conjured for itself. When we rescued her, the chair she was strapped to had a nightmare assortment of steel appendages springing up from underneath. Maybe it's better she *doesn't* remember that. But this confused state is no good, either. She can't find her mate that way. I didn't know the person she was before, but her dragon spirit is *strong* —she's fighting to get better every day—and I know she'd be happier as a mated dragon. She and her mate both have half of a soul. It's part of her destiny.

As a dragon myself, I can speak to the loneliness of not fulfilling that destiny. Dragons weren't meant to go two hundred years without mating. Eventually, our bodies give up the fight, but our hearts break long before that. A female dragon spirit will continue to be reborn, continue to seek her mate across centuries, but once the male dragon dies, her dragon spirit will pass with him. It's possible that Cinder's soul mate has already passed—maybe he was one of the *withered* we've lost recently. A new dragon seems to succumb every few weeks. But I feel certain her mate is still alive. I can't be sure, but I just *feel* like her dragon spirit is still kicking, still hungering for her mate, which means her mate is out there somewhere.

I made a promise to help her heal and find him. And if he's already gone, then I could do a lot worse than spend what's left of my days in the company of someone as beautiful and strong as Cinder Dubois. Even as a friend, if that's all we can be.

I take one last, long breath of the perfumed air, then I turn back to the cottage.

Back inside, Cinder and Biti are halfway to the bed. "Got some fresh lilies for you!" I say brightly, sweeping ahead of them to swap out the tired stems from two days ago. The vase sits on a table next to the bed, where her lunch is already waiting. Normally, honeymooners have the cottage to themselves, but we've brought in an entire staff to make sure Cinder's cared for 24/7—cook and housekeeper, nurses in shifts. I sleep on the couch in the living room and shower in the second bathroom. Nikolais brings me fresh clothes. It's a whole operation.

I step back so she can see the flowers, and she's entranced, just like the last time. Biti lets her walk the few steps by herself to the table. Cinder's eyes are wide, looking at me, not speaking but searching my face.

"Go ahead, they're for you." I smile. "The food, too. It's time for lunch." I say it with enthusiasm, hoping she'll actually eat.

She cups the flowers with her thin-fingered hands and bends to put her face nose-deep into the fiery-orange Tigerlily blossoms. One sleeve of her nightgown slides down her shoulder. She doesn't fix it, just straightens and says in a whisper, without looking back, "Thank you. They smell so nice."

"My pleasure." I exchange a brief, hopeful look with Biti—those are the most words strung together we've heard from her yet.

"I'll leave you to lunch, then." Biti encourages me with a flourish of her hands as she retreats from the room.

I step up behind Cinder and gently lift her sleeve back into place. "Would you like to sit for lunch?" I gesture to the chair where I was sitting before—I've eaten plenty of meals there—but she just shuffles back to the bed. I'd help her get in, but she manages it without me. Which is good. "Alright, the bed, then!" I trot across the room to retrieve the swing tray, the one that goes over the bed so she can eat there. With a flourish, I present her with a plate of grilled cheese and berries. She picks up one berry and puts it in her mouth. While she gets started on that, I take a seat and text her sister.

CINDER'S UP AND EATING. AND TALKING (SOME). GOOD TIME TO VISIT.

It takes a few seconds, then the reply comes back. TWO MINUTES.

COME IN THE NORMAL WAY. The last thing Cinder needs is her sister teleporting straight into the room.

When I look up, the berries are gone, and Cinder's eating the sandwich with two hands. "How about some milk with that?" I spring up from my seat.

She blinks—too much—but nods as she chews. I have to peel off the extensive plastic the chef has wrapped around the cup, but I finally get it free. By the time I get it to her, she's downed half the sandwich. Which is *tremendous.* So many good signs. I hand the milk to her. She closes her eyes and tips her head back to drink it. She's gulping it down like she's parched.

The need to simply *talk* starts me babbling. "The chef will make you anything you like. He put some sun tea on the front step yesterday—it's probably ready by now. And there are more berries, I'm sure. Would you like some more?"

She's finished drinking, setting down her cup on the tray with an extreme level of care. She has an adorable milk mustache I just want to reach over and wipe off, but that wouldn't be cool. I take a seat instead. She's not saying anything, just frowning at the tray and blinking.

"That's fine." My heart's kind of sinking. "We'll try it next time. Maybe for dinner." I shut my mouth because my throat is closing up.

She slowly turns and squints at me. "Everything's… fuzzy." The words take great effort.

"I know." I slide to the front of my chair. I want to go to her, hold her hand. "It's going to be okay. You just need a little time." I'm dying to close the distance between the chair and the bed and hold her hand—like I did when she was feverish. Back then, it didn't seem to matter. She was so confused, couldn't focus… touch was the only thing that soothed her. That, and my voice whispering reassurances in her ear as she thrashed. Now she's awake enough to know that she *doesn't* know me—or at least doesn't remember me—and that makes everything harder.

She nods with my words, but that seems to draw her eyelids down. Before I can think of something else to say, she's slumping her head back—only the pillow's in the wrong place, and the head of the bed is raised too much for sleeping. I spring up and push the button to lower the bed, then reach behind her to hold her up while I adjust the pillow.

When I do, her eyes open again, and she gazes blearily up at me. "You take care of me."

"Yes, I do." We're close enough I can feel her breath on my chest. "There you go." The head of the bed is down now, and the pillow is in a comfortable spot. She settles into it and closes her eyes.

I step back, uncertain about what to do now. Take away the tray?

"Thank you. Aleks." She breathes out my name, and I'm riveted.

"*My pleasure,*" I whisper. I don't know if she can even hear me.

She answers with a sigh.

A few seconds later, the door opens, and Cinder's twin sister, Ember, comes hurrying through. I put my finger to my lips. She grimaces when she sees Cinder with her eyes closed. This isn't the first time she's not been able to get here before Cinder lapsed back into sleep. I wave Ember back into the hallway outside the room and follow her out.

Biti looks up from her computer expectantly.

I close the door, so we won't wake Cinder. "She's worn out," I say to both. "But she did eat, so that's good."

Ember's still disappointed. "You said she was

talking. Did she say anything about how she was captured? Or what they did? Maybe something about the witch?"

I shake my head and try not to scowl. I know everyone wants to know what happened while Cinder was captured by the Vardigah... and whether the witch who helped us escape will send the Vardigah after her.

"She's just not there yet," I say.

Ember looks to the closed door. The worry on her face digs into me. I know it's hard to watch her sister in this state. I don't even know Cinder, not really—we've just had this connection since she's been back—and I worry. Her twin sister has to be distraught. Nikolais said something about blaming herself for Cinder being captured, which is crazy. The witch has to be the one who found Cinder— that's literally what witches *do*. Well, *did*. When they were still around. Which hasn't been for two hundred years, so who knows. But it's not Ember's fault—everyone but her recognizes that.

"You want to sit with her a while?" I offer.

"No. I mean, if she's still sleeping..." She kind of shrugs, helpless. Tormented.

I just nod.

"Let me know when she wakes up again." Ember scowls. "I'll get here faster next time."

I nod again, and she says goodbye to Biti then walks toward the front. She'll teleport as soon as she's out of sight, but the mated dragons try not to do that in front of the staff.

"She cares for her sister," Biti says. "Too much, probably."

"I know." I gesture to the door. "I'll be inside."

She goes back to whatever she was doing on the computer.

I clear out the lunch stuff, spend a little time on the balcony in the sun, text an update on the situation to Niko, then catch up on some stuff on my phone. By the time I settle back into my chair inside, Cinder's having a dream—arms twitching a little, eyes moving fast under their lids. I put the phone away and watch. She's beautiful to look at, even when she's asleep, but I can almost see the drama of her dreams unfold. The harsh intakes of breath. The sudden movement of limbs. There's an ebb-and-flow to the story going on inside her mind, a drama that fills her unconscious state—I wish she could tell me what it was when she wakes up. Sometimes, she thrashes awake. Then she's frantic. I like to be there for that, soothing her, like I did during the feverish times.

So I'm somewhat alert and waiting when she startles the hell out of me.

"*No!*" It's mostly a gasp, but I still jump inside my skin and nearly fall out of my chair. She bolts straight up in her bed.

I scramble to my feet and lurch to the bedside. "It's okay." I reach for her then pull back when her eyes pop open, and she swings sharply at the sound of my voice.

She's still breathing hard from the sudden wake-up, but she's furiously scanning my face, frowning hard, but with a sharpness I've never seen. "You're Aleks, right?"

My heart skips a beat. "Yeah."

She quickly scours the room with her gaze then comes back. "What is this place? And how long have I been out?"

I'm stunned out of words.

TWO

Cinder

NOTHING MAKES ANY SENSE.

A gorgeous guy who I somehow know is named Aleks but that I know nothing else about is gaping at me like I'm an alien. I have no idea where I am, and no memory of getting here. And speaking of aliens, the last thing I remember is one abducting me from my bedroom in my apartment, which is clearly some dream/hallucination, and now I'm *here.* "Here" being a strangely beautiful hospital suite, judging by the flowers, bed in the middle of the room, and a bank of medical monitoring equipment at my bedside.

This Aleks person is giving me the strangest looks—and not answering my questions.

"Okay, I'm just going to…" I fight with the

covers to get my legs out. They feel weak, but I don't let that slow me down. "I'll see my way out—"

"Wait!" Aleks throws his hands up to block me. "Cinder, you can't just—"

He cuts off at my fierce look. This guy better not try to stop me. I'm halfway out of the bed. The stone floor is cool on my bare feet. I'm wearing a *nightgown. Shit.* I scowl at him. "You can't keep me here." But a sudden wave of weakness runs through my body. What's wrong with me?

"It's not like that." His hands are still up, but his eyes are pleading with me. And he's got beautiful eyes. Light gray with dark rims. Thick lashes. Dark brows that are just a bit wild. Messy. He has the kind of eyes I would love to capture on film… in a barely lit room with just a beam of illumination across his face. The rest of him is beautiful, too, but those eyes… *fuck.* Why am I thinking about shoots?

I swallow and edge back on the bed, gripping the mattress. The sheets are luxury-soft while the bed is ultra-firm. I give the place another look. Hospital. High-end. Beautiful man making sure I don't get out of bed. Because… why?

"Oh, God, I've done something." It's a whisper, but it shrinks me further onto the bed.

"What? No." He frowns and lowers his hands. "I just don't want you to get up too quickly. You've… you've been out for a while."

He's hedging. Fear trickles through me. Did I go through with it? Did I try and just… *forget?* Block it out? I swallow down the creeping horror of that and turn over my hands, checking my wrists. No bandages. No scars from slashes across them. I put a hand to my neck, but I don't feel anything there, either.

I look up at this guy, Aleks. He's super concerned. He's wearing something that looks like scrubs. He's a doctor or nurse or something. "Was it drugs, then?" I ask, weakly. I'm feeling light-headed all of a sudden. I blink to ward off the fuzzy-headedness.

"What do you mean?" His voice is so soft. Gentle. The way you talk to someone you're afraid is on the edge of a breakdown. Or fragile and frightened like an injured wild animal.

I straighten, so he knows I'm not crazy. Or weak. I'm just… *confused.* "Did I try to kill myself with pills?" I keep my voice blunt. I just want to know the truth.

"*What?* No. I mean…" His concern rockets through the roof. "Why would you think that?"

Well, *shit.* I'm not explaining all that to some guy I don't even know. Although that thought tugs at my heart because somehow, I feel like I *do* know him. *Aleks.* I knew his name. How? My memory's a blank from my apartment to here. And I've never seen this guy before. Except he's *here* and he seems to know me. *Something* happened.

"Okay, Aleks, look…" I gesture to the whole place like the mystery it is. I just now notice there's a beautiful view over a balcony. Floor-to-ceiling windows showcase a garden and trees and water beyond. I am *not* in the city, that's for sure. "I need some explanation here because I don't understand *anything* about this."

A smile flashes across his face.

"What?" I snap.

"I've just… I've been waiting a while for you to say something like that." He seems overly excited.

Oh, God. "How long have I been here?"

"Two weeks." He says it quickly, so I guess I believe him.

But God… *two weeks?* "What happened?" What happened *to me.* Because something obviously terrible happened for me to lose time and location… and if I didn't try to kill myself…

His smile evaporates. "What do you remember?"

"I remember *nothing, Aleks!*" Anger surges up, raw and ragged. I dig in a tighter grip on the mattress because the emotion makes me dizzy. I squeeze my eyes shut, trying to focus. "I remember being in my apartment. For days. A week, maybe? I... I can't remember what the last thing was..." I open my eyes. Aleks's have gone wide. "My sister. I remember we had... we talked. She was the last person I remember talking to." *We fought.* It was half-hearted because we never fight, and I was just... I had to quit the project. So we fought as much as we ever do, and I ran back to my place and slowly sank into a deeper, darker place than I already was. "And now I'm *here,*" I say pointedly to Aleks. I leave out the alien coming to my bedroom to abduct me because that's obviously some bizarre dream I had in between. "So what the fuck happened? How am I here? And what is this place?" *Hospital.* I know it is. I just need him to talk so the feeling of not quite having a grip on reality will recede.

"Okay. I'll explain." He's back to that soothing voice. "But it's kind of a lot to take in and... we should take it slow. Okay?"

I'm feeling jittery, and that sense of *weakness* washes over me again. "Slow. Okay."

He steps a little closer. "How about if we go out on the balcony for a bit? You haven't been outside for a couple weeks. Maybe it'll be... less... strange?"

I don't know why it would matter. *All* of this is strange. But he's got this soft look in his eyes, and he's not trying to force me into anything. I'm in a fucking *nightgown,* and he's not creepy or weird about that. He's just being... *nice.* And he seems genuinely concerned.

"All right." I put my feet down on the cool floor again and rise up from the bed. "Is there some-where to sit out there? I'm not super steady."

He's instantly by my side, taking my arm and slipping his hand to the small of my back. "Abso-lutely," he says, supporting me with what feels like a mountain of muscle in a velvet grip. I mean, he's *solid.*

I flick a look at him—because he's awfully *close* —but he seems entirely wrapped up in making sure I'm not going to splat on the stone floor. And I'm not steady, so I allow it. I focus instead on my legs, which seem way too freaking wobbly. As we shuffle toward the door to the balcony, I feel a little stronger. Like maybe my body is just waking up. Have I been in a coma? Maybe I got in a car wreck, and that wiped out my memory, and I've been out ever since. But I see no injuries. Two weeks isn't long to recover from something major. Maybe I just hit my head?

"I'm good," I say as we get close to the balcony door, waving him off from having to keep me locked in his mountain-of-muscle grip.

He looks uncertain, but then he lets me walk on my own while he scuttles over and slides open the door. There's a small couch on the balcony and some steps to go down to the garden. I'm very much not ready for the steps, so I brace myself on the glass door and use that to work my way across the couch. Finally, I ease into it—not because I'm achy, although that too, but because I'm not sure my legs won't buckle under me. Once I'm down, I relax again, and then it hits me—*the smell.* The mingled fragrance of a dozen types of flowers in the garden floats up and bathes me in calm. The sun is bright but not too much—the balcony has an overhang that gives us shade—and the beauty of the garden and fountain and the sparkling water beyond is soothing just like Aleks said it would be.

"This is nice." I lean back into the cushions.

Aleks smiles, and I don't think I've ever seen a man so happy from three little words that weren't *I love you.* Or maybe *please fuck me.* That thought makes me blush. Not because I think Aleks secretly wants to fuck me—where in the world did that idea come from?—but because his smile is so *pure* that I feel bad for tainting it with naughty thoughts.

"Okay, I'm sitting down," I say. "The garden is amazing. This is kind of a slice of heaven right here, isn't it?" I have a sudden ache for my camera, the second time in minutes, when before I landed in this place, the idea of ever touching one again made me want to vomit. This place *is* magical.

"It really is," Aleks says, but it makes me blush in a different way because he's not looking at the garden at all. He's giving me sexy puppy eyes and, *my God,* I'm a sucker for a gorgeous pair of eyes.

I twist to face him. "So tell me. How bad is it?"

He draws in a breath and bites his lip. "Well, you don't remember the past couple weeks, so I'm going with *pretty bad.*" He frowns and hesitates. "You've been in some kind of strange, feverish state like you were fighting off a virus, only the doctors couldn't find anything wrong. Just a little while ago, you told me you felt everything was *fuzzy.*"

My self-conscious nature squishes up. "I *talked* to

you?" Oh, God, what did I say? "I don't remember any of that."

"You didn't say much." He smiles, but it's a little pained. "I think you were struggling to come back, but your mind was protecting you from something. Like… maybe it didn't want to remember, so you didn't. And now…" He gestures to this rather pathetic state I'm in.

"Now I can't remember anything." But it's not true. I remember *everything* that sent me spiraling down in the first place. I *wish* I could forget the young girls Ember and I found malnourished and beaten in a trailer overseas. They were kept like animals for the men who wanted to rape them. Their stories, as Ember talked to them, sometimes on camera, sometimes not, tore me apart. Then when we came back to the States, and it was worse—

"Maybe it's better if you don't," Aleks says, peering at me.

"If I don't what?"

"Remember."

I squeeze my eyes shut and shake my head. "You don't understand. I *do* remember." I open my eyes to find him transfixed. I look away, out at the sparkling blue of the water beyond the brilliant green canopy of the trees. There are a million shots I could take of this place, and none would have little girls whose bodies had been violated; whose minds had been destroyed; and whose lives had been snuffed out. "I don't know what's happened for the last two weeks, but I wasn't in a good place before that. And I remember that just fine." I drag my gaze over to him. "But you don't need to hear about that."

"Maybe it would help to talk about it." He's got those kindly eyes out again.

"What is this place? Psych hospital? Are you my therapist?"

He huffs a laugh. "Not even close." His humor settles a little. "It's complicated, but basically, a friend of your sister owns this place. He said you could stay here as long as you needed. She thought it would be a good place for you while you were, well, struggling. We weren't sure what was going on with you. She's going to be very excited to see you like this."

I cringe a little. I'm not sure I'm ready to see Ember just yet. "What does that make you? My personal nurse?" That sounds naughtier than I meant it, and I'm back to having heat in my cheeks, but thankfully, Aleks doesn't take it that way. I think.

He just smiles sweetly. "I'm a volunteer."

I nod.

He props his arm on the back of the couch like he's settling in. "But if you want someone to talk to about…" He waves his hand. "…this *not good* place you were in before, I'm all ears. Promise it'll stay between us."

I frown because that's the last thing I want to talk about. But I'm missing a couple weeks of my life, and no one knows what I was going through. Well, Ember has a clue, but she's not the kind to understand this. This guy—this soft-hearted guy who volunteers to take care of quasi-coma patients —he'll probably understand. He feels… *safe* somehow.

I drop my gaze to the couch cushion, which is a plastic-y outdoor-proof fabric, and I play with the edge. "I was working on a documentary with my sister. It was about sex trafficking. Mostly underage kids." I peek to check if he's freaked out by this, but his gray eyes are just wide and solemn. "My sister's the strong one," I add.

"If you mean strong-willed, then yes." He has a small smile now.

"Ah, you've met her. Of course." I look away and shift a little in my seat. If Aleks has met Ember, then he knows how true that is—that I've always been the softer twin. The one that's too sensitive. Too easily crushed. Ember would move mountains, and I would be off picking dandelions. "Right. So, of course, Ember wants to save the world—because that's what she does—and she needed a female cameraperson, so I came along for the ride." I look back to Aleks. "It's rough. Seeing all that stuff. Even from behind the camera."

His brow wrinkles up, but in concern, not judgment.

"Anyway, we went on this one bust with the police." I swallow down the sudden dryness in my throat. Even as I say the words, the images come flooding back. The smell of blood. Of gunpowder. "We were supposed to just follow them in—Ember first, me trailing with the camera. It was an old farmhouse with lots of rooms. They were holding the girls in the basement. In a cage. It was… awful." I'm staring out at the water now. The beautiful, sparkling water, but all I can see is the dark wood paneling between the bars of the cage that held a dozen girls, packed in like animals. "The buyers would come to the house. The traffickers would bring the assigned girl up from the basement. Then they'd lock her in a room until the buyer was done. We thought the police had cleared all the rooms. They had the traffickers in cuffs outside. They were calling in paramedics to bring in the girls. Ember wanted to talk to one of them—a sweet little red-haired girl, so tiny, but Ember thought she was strong enough to go on camera. Only my sister didn't want me filming yet or even in the room." My gaze wanders away from the water to find Aleks looking devastated—like he was right there with me. It stabs me with guilt. "You don't need to hear this."

"Yes, I do," he says softly. Then he takes my hand, which is lying limp in my lap, and holds it, so gently. Yet strong. Like if I was dangling off a cliff, and Aleks had a hold of me, I know he would save me.

So I keep going, staring at his hand around mine because I can't look in those pretty eyes while I tell the rest. "So I just get some walking shots. Going through the house. Opening the doors. Footage of the rooms." My voice catches a little, but I breathe through it. "I opened one, and there was a buyer inside with one of the girls. They were being quiet. That's the only thing I can figure. They were quiet because he thought he might get away with it —*with her*—if he just kept everything... *quiet*. She was so young. And terrified. He was holding her tight with his hand over her mouth. I was leading with my camera, so I saw everything through that rectangular frame…" I hold up my hand and make a corner of the frame and peer through it. I can see it now. Perfectly staged because I was absolutely frozen in place. Frozen and useless. "He had a gun. I didn't see the gun. All I saw was his hand over her mouth and her big brown eyes, wide and terrified. But he had a gun, and he shot her right through the head."

I stop.

Time feels empty for a moment.

Just like back then, in that suspended second of time, when I stood there and did nothing, camera rolling as he killed a little girl in front of me.

"*Cinder.* I'm so… sorry." His voice pulls me back —out of that room, out of the frame of my hand, back to this little garden paradise. I look at him, and he has tears running down his face.

"*Oh, Aleks.*" I wipe away his tears. On both cheeks, with my thumbs as I hold his face. He just lets me, and his eyes are the most beautiful thing I've ever seen—darker gray now, sparkling with tears, lashes wet. "I'm sorry," I whisper. "I shouldn't have told you." But there's something about his tears on my hands—they tingle on my skin. *So strange.*

"That doesn't matter." He takes my hands, both of them, and holds them between his. Between us. "So this is what haunted you."

"I did nothing." The grimace makes my face hurt.

His brow scrunches up. "What could you have done?"

"Stop filming? Call for help?" I've thought about this a million times. "Thrown my fucking camera at him? Those things are heavy. I could have shoved my camera right in his face and at least... *done something.* A delay of even a half second could have saved her."

Aleks shakes his head. "He could have shot you."

I give him a look, then huff a laugh and pull my hands from between his. "He tried to."

"Oh, *shit.* Really?" Now he's even more concerned.

Which is funny because there have been plenty of times I've wished he would have shot me first. "He shot *at* me. He tried shooting down the hall. Couldn't hit a damn thing. He even tried to shoot himself, but the fucker was so dumb, he'd run out of bullets by that point." I shake my head. "The police came and got him after that. But the girl was already dead." I stare out at the water again. "Her name was Candace."

After a moment, he asks, "Is that why you were thinking of suicide?"

I lift my eyebrows and give him a tight smile. "Don't tell Ember that, okay?"

"Promise," he vows, and it's like he's swearing it on his grandmother's grave.

I shake my head. "I put down the camera. Right there in that room. And walked away. I told Ember I couldn't keep working on the project. Then I went home and got really fucking drunk. For about a day. I sobered up, but it didn't get any better. I never wanted to touch a camera again. And photography has been my life since I was… I don't even know. Young." I look back to him. "It was a pretty dark time. And, I mean, I *thought* about maybe ending the pain, once or twice, but I didn't do anything about it. Or maybe I did."

He scowls. "What do you mean?"

"I mean, I gave myself this fucking amnesia. Or something. My body shut down, and I can't remember the last couple weeks, and now I'm here.

So I guess I just found a creative way to block every-thing out?"

He's biting his lip again. "That's not what happened."

Now it's my turn to scowl. "I thought you said—"

"I said it was complicated." He's frowning. "And I'm not sure this is the best time to tell you."

"I mean…" I gesture around us with both hands. "Is there a better time?"

"I guess not." He sucks in air between his teeth. "You were kidnapped by a magical race of dark elves. They're called the Vardigah—"

I lurch away from him on the couch. "Shut the fuck up."

"I know it sounds crazy but—"

"I was *not* kidnapped. By fucking *aliens*. I was *not.*" Panic vibrates my body. I'm hunched as far away from him on the couch as I can get.

"Well, they're not aliens… I mean, I guess…"

I shove a finger in his face. *"No!"* Then I scramble up on my feet, using handholds wherever I can—his shoulder, back of the couch, the glass wall—in a desperate bid to move, run, escape…

"Cinder, wait!"

I stumble back into the room, my feet slapping against the stone tiles. I'm barely staying upright, but I reach the bed, use it to stay up by bracing my way around, then I spy a door. I head for it, reaching it just before Aleks reaches me, his protests lost in the roar going on in my brain. I fling the door open and rush out. *All of this is a dream.* It has to be. I haven't woken up. I'm still in a coma having an insane dream about beautiful orderlies with gray eyes and soft hearts telling me I've been abducted by aliens—

"Ms. Cinder!" a small Indian woman proclaims.

It surprises me enough, I lose my footing. I'm falling for a split second, then Aleks has me, scooping me somehow out of thin air. His hands are like iron bands clamped onto my upper arms, then he wraps his arms around me, holding me gently to his chest. He's mumbling something about being sorry, but the panic is making my heart beat out of my chest.

"Just come back to the bed," he says, then mumbles some more things.

The sound of his voice, the smooth strength of his touch works a strange magic on me. The panicked fluttering of my heart slows. I can breathe again, at least a little. I let him turn me around and lead me back into the room because I simply have no energy left to resist. He lifts me into the bed.

"I'm so sorry," he says, over and over, smoothing my hair and the blankets and turning his worried gray eyes to me. I just gaze into them, no energy for words, until the fatigue pulls me down, and my eyelids slowly drop closed.

THREE

Aleksandr

WHAT THE FUCK DID I *DO?*

Cinder fell asleep *hard* after I basically fucked up everything. I texted Niko in a panic, and he came right away, but she was out cold, and even me relaying the whole thing, and not in a whisper, didn't wake her. He left to bring Ember up to speed. I stayed and waited anxiously for Cinder to wake up again. She didn't.

For going on twelve hours now.

A few times, she mumbled and turned over, but that was it. I went to grab some sleep on the couch in the great room, giving the night staff strict instructions to get me if she awoke, but they never did... and I slept through until morning. After checking on her, I hurried through a shower, but she was still sleeping. Now I'm pacing her room, waiting, hoping… and kicking myself for rushing her. What the hell was I thinking? Magical race of dark elves? For fuck's sake. I *know* that's not how you introduce a potential soul mate to our world. I was just so swept up in her story, her beautiful, tormented face, the tremble in her hands when I held them… and that is zero fucking excuse.

As soon as she wakes, we've all agreed—we're bringing in Ember. And I pray her sister can fix the damage I've done.

Cinder makes another murmuring sound, and I almost miss it with my incessant pacing and the berating mantra in my head. I freeze when she stretches and makes quiet noises like she's awake. My phone is out a half-second later, and I text Niko, SHE'S UP. He'll get Ember here in a flash. I stow it and keep my distance. I'm practically by the door to the balcony. Should I slip out? Would it be better to have no one—

"You," she says sleepily, struggling up to sitting.

My heart lurches. "Hi." *Hi?* Fuck.

She frowns and looks around. "You're still here."

"Yeah. I um…" I'm choking on the severe need to *not* speak. But it's *huge* that she's awake and aware

—relief trickles through me. At least I didn't send her back into that horrible state from before. An awkward silence stretches while she scrutinizes me —then suddenly the door swings open and her sister strides in. *Thank God.* Niko's right behind her.

"Cinder?" Ember rushes across the room. *"Holy shit,* it's good to see you awake." She sweeps Cinder up in a hug. Am I the only one who senses Cinder's hesitation? Niko has to see her slightly panicked look. But I'm determined to stay silent and out of the way, so I don't fuck up anything more. I'd disappear if I could, but slipping out now would just draw attention to myself.

Ember releases her from their fierce embrace and settles on the bed next to her. It's so strange to see the two, side by side. Identical twins, although I can easily tell the difference. Ember has a tiny dot birthmark on her face, for one. And Cinder's face has a more roundness to it. A gentleness that I think reflects her heart, now that I've gotten to know her a little. Although that will probably be the extent of it—it's up to Ember to bring her into the reality of the situation now.

Cinder flicks a look to me then back to her sister. "I think maybe you should pinch me."

Ember cocks her head. "Okay, what?"

"Just to make sure I'm awake this time." She looks at me again.

My heart hammers as all three look my way. "Maybe I should go?" I hook a thumb behind me to the glass door. I fumble for the handle.

"Aleks, it's all right." Niko beckons me over with a wave of his hand. "You should be part of this."

I really *shouldn't* but... I drag my ass across the floor, giving Niko a look that says, *I don't give a flying fuck if you're the Lord of the Lair, this is fucking stupid.* He glares back, and I force a smile on my face and stop near the end of the bed.

Cinder gives me a crooked look then says, "You weren't this awkward in my dream." Then she frowns and turns to Ember. "Unless that wasn't a dream, in which case, your hot volunteer says some crazy things. You might want to check that out." She scrunches up her face.

Ember's lips are pressed tight. Niko gives her an encouraging nod. She turns back to her sister. "How're you feeling?"

"Better." Cinder nods to back that up. "Like my head's finally clearing out."

"That's good. *Great.*" Ember glances at me. "Aleks said you didn't remember anything from the last two weeks. Still true?"

"Yeah. But you need to tell me straight, Em—what the hell happened to me?"

"I *want* to tell you, sis."

Cinder squints. "It's bad, isn't it? Am I dying? Cancer? What? I swear I've thought of all the horrible things it can be, okay? I'm not a fragile flower."

"No one thinks that," Niko throws in.

Cinder peers up at him, then back at Ember. "Okay, he's pretty hot. Obviously intelligent, too. I approve."

Ember cracks a smile. "Good to know." She takes Niko's hand. "Niko, meet Cinder. She's my sister."

"I noticed a family resemblance." He extends his hand. "Pleased to make your acquaintance, Ms. Dubois."

Cinder shakes his hand, smirks, then fake-whispers, "He's a comedian, too."

Ember's smile tempers. "And my soul mate."

Cinder leans back. "Whoa! Okay, that's... intense." She lifts an eyebrow. "All that happened while I was sleeping in his fancy hospital? Am I like a great matchmaker, or what?"

Niko grins, and Ember snorts a laugh. "More than you know."

"Yeah, well, I don't know *jack.*" Cinder fake-scowls. "This is where you fill me in."

Ember's back to frowning. She flicks a look at me, but she'd have to torture words out of my mouth at this point. To Cinder, she says, "Okay. Here's the thing. The world is far crazier than you know."

Cinder narrows her eyes. "If you say anything about aliens, I'm going back to bed and starting over again."

"Not aliens." Ember hesitates then takes hold of her sister's wrist—the one with the jagged half-circle birthmark—and lays her own next to it. They're upside down to each other, so they don't match, but even I can see that they're identical. "Remember what we said about this when we were kids?"

"That they were sister tattoos…" Cinder starts.

"…except the tattooist was drunk," Ember finishes. "Because they're supposed to fit together, but they don't." She looks Cinder in the eyes. "What did we decide later?"

Cinder's eyes go wide, and she dashes a look at Niko. "No fucking way."

"What?" Niko asks. He's as wrapped up in this as I am—I edge forward slightly until I'm at the foot of the bed. No one notices.

Ember gives her sister a nod to go on.

Cinder's got a small smile. "That there were two twin boys out there—hot boys, mind you—that had the other halves. That someday we would find them and have a double wedding." She leans forward, eyes alight. *"Please* tell me there's another one for me."

"In a way." Ember's biting her lip.

Niko's smug look makes me want to punch him. This code talk of soul mates is twisting my stomach. Because I know she has one, and the odds are about 100:1 of it being me. And I know I vowed to help her find her one-and-only mate, but that was before she woke up and looked at me with those amber-green eyes.

Cinder leans back, her beautiful eyes bugging out. "Oh, *get out.* This is too weird." She scans Niko's arms—his dress shirt sleeves are rolled up to bare his forearms. There's clearly no tattoo, but I already knew that. "Does he have the birthmark and everything? Because that would be too much."

"It's much stranger than that," Ember says carefully. She waits until Cinder catches the seriousness of her tone.

"Okay, tell me."

Ember takes her sister's hands in hers. "Don't

freak on me, okay? No running away. No… shutting me out, all right? Because this is important. And I about lost my mind when I couldn't find you."

Cinder frowns. "You couldn't find me?"

Ember squeezes her sister's hands. "Promise me."

"Okay, I promise. Sheesh." But she's tossing wary looks at Niko and me now.

Ember pulls in a breath and lets it out slowly. "Niko and his people are shapeshifters. They can turn into dragons. The birthmarks? They mean we're destined to be their soul mates."

Cinder just blinks. And stares. And blinks again. "That's not funny, Em."

"Okay, I'm going to show you." Ember stands up from the bed and steps back. Niko gives her room by shuffling over next to me at the end of the bed.

"What?" Cinder's alarm jumps up.

Holy shit. Ember's not going to—

She does. She shifts right in front of Cinder. Her dragon form is brilliant gold and takes up every inch of the room between the door and the bed.

"Holy fuck!" Cinder shrieks and jerks to the side in her hospital bed, away from her sister's dragon. Being tangled up in the sheets seems to be the only

thing keeping her from scrambling out the side of the bed.

In a flash, Cinder shifts back. Except she's naked. *Shit.* I look away at the same time Niko blocks my view. Not before I saw pretty much everything, though. And I can't help imagining that's what Cinder looks like without the nightgown.

"What. The. Fuck!" Cinder yells at her sister. "Are you kidding me?"

"Well, you wouldn't believe me if I didn't!" Ember yells back.

"You are not— That was not— *Fuck!"*

"Just… let me… get my clothes on." I hear Ember's bare feet pad across the floor and, when I look, Cinder's up on her knees in bed, with the sheets gathered to her chin. Ember clambers onto the bed and grabs hold of her shoulders. "Don't freak on me!"

Cinder twists out of her hold and falls back on her butt. "Don't tell me what to do!"

"Like I *ever* tell you what to do!" Ember's fists are shaking at her side.

"What? You're *always* telling me what to do! *Fuck,* Ember! *What the hell?"*

Niko lands a heavy hand on my shoulder and leans in. "Time for us to go."

"But—" I'm cut off by the screaming match.

"How was I *supposed* to convince you?" Ember's looming over Cinder, who's defiantly shaking her fists at her sister while still knocked back on her butt.

"I don't know. Not *that!*"

On second thought, I give Niko a nod, and we haul it out of the room. I don't think the women even noticed. Biti is wide-eyed in the hall. "Is everything all right?"

I give her a helpless shrug. "Sisters?"

She nods sagely but gives a skeptical look to the closed door. We can all hear the shouting, but the words aren't distinct. I can't tell if they're settling or if it's more quiet because the door is closed.

Niko steers me down the hall toward the great room. "Let's let them work it out."

I couldn't agree more. Cinder's not freaking out, not the way she did with me. She's not collapsing again. She's up and fighting—like that Dragon Spirit I know she has—and that's just what she needs to get through this. I suddenly realize that might have been the plan all along.

Once we're around the corner, I say, "You could have let me leave sooner, you know."

Niko wipes his face with his hand like he just

escaped a harrowing house fire. "You needed to see that." He quickly adds, "Cinder's shock not Ember's naked body."

"I didn't see a thing."

Niko snorts. "Cinder's going to be okay. I wanted you to know it wasn't your fault she retreated. I think Ember might be the only one who can really reach her right now."

I glance back at the hall. "If they don't kill each other."

He smiles. "I think they're pretty evenly matched." Then he gets serious. "You don't need to stay by her side anymore, Aleks. You can go home."

My chest squeezes. "I don't mind."

He cocks his head and puts his hand on my shoulder. "I see how you look at her, my brother. But she might not be yours. *Aleks.* Probably not."

"Doesn't matter."

"The hell it doesn't." His expression darkens. "I don't want you broken-hearted when she finds her mate."

"My heart's been broken for at least fifty years." But I lighten my tone in a desperate bid to not have Niko send me away. "What's another chunk ripped out and stomped by a beautiful mate who's not mine?" I'm talking about Shujin, of course. She's mated now to Rhox, but before they discovered they were soul mates, I was smitten with her. Half the lair was, but I was the one who brought her in. Found her down in New York City, fighting on the streets, and I helped to fend off her attackers. Not that she needed me, but it gave me a chance to befriend her. It took some time before I could convince her to come to the lair. I was the first to reveal myself to her. The first to romance her into a True Kiss. And the first to discover she wasn't my other half. It was decades ago, but it was the closest I'd come to falling for someone I thought might truly be my mate. There were others, but I was never in love with them *before* the first kiss. Before I knew she wasn't *the one*, and that our love would be destined to be a mere fling, maybe even a serious one, as I waited. *Always waiting.* That was me... and Niko.

And now just me.

Niko squeezes my shoulder. "Go back to the lair. Get some real rest. You can come back and visit when things are more, well, settled."

The sound of the fighting down the hall calms. Which doesn't mean I'd be welcome back there—in fact, it means Ember probably succeeded where I failed. Bringing someone into our world is never easy. And I was just far too eager to be the one.

"All right." I force myself to turn and walk out the front door of the cottage.

It feels like I'm ripping out a part of my heart anyway.

FOUR

Cinder

THE WORLD IS *NUTS*... BUT I DON'T THINK I AM.

Ember has convinced me of that if nothing else.

And she brought me real clothes—although they're very *extra*. A yellow designer skirt that feels like a whisper around my legs, it's so weightless, and a silky white blouse that's way too fancy for being in a hospital. Or rehab. Whatever this is. Her rich boyfriend is supplying all the stuff, so I really can't complain, and it does make me feel less like I'm in an institution.

Although, I should probably be committed to one for believing dragons are real.

It's been a couple days, so the idea is settling in. Ember's told me all about Niko's secret people, their fight with these freaky creatures who kidnapped me

—which I still don't remember except that snippet when I first got taken—and this whole idea about soul mates. All of it is completely nuts. And yet... apparently, also true. At least the part where my sister has turned into a shape-shifting dragon and is working on making a dragon baby. The idea that *Ember*—my globe-trotting, super-career-oriented sister—is on the fast track to making a baby with a guy she just met is *also* crazy. Although, if I'm honest, it fits. It's always been all-or-nothing with my twin. I just thought I'd be the first to reach the family-making stage. Figures she would beat me there, too.

I love my sister, I truly do—she's just a little *extra* sometimes as well.

I breathe in the perfume of the flowers and get the swing going with a push of my toes. The pavement is heating up in the morning sun, and it might be tricky getting back to the room without burning my soles. The pergola gives me some shade for now. The distant sound of the water birds and the wind in the trees is like a meditation tape, and the simple beauty of the garden feels like it's filling up my soul. I grip the back of the wooden-plank bench-swing and give another push, swinging to the limits the chains will allow. A chipmunk scampers into the shade with me, goes up on its hind legs, and pauses with a seed in its paws, evaluating whether I'm friend or foe. I ache for a camera to snap his perfect little ears, tiny fingers, and racing-stripe back. I settle for a mental snapshot before he twitches his tail and dashes off into the broad-leafed ferns around the pergola.

Something so perfect and mundane is just what I need right now amid the crazy.

I hear the sliding door of the cottage open, but even with shading my eyes, I can't make out who it is—there's too much glare off the glass. "Biti, I'll come up there for lunch," I call out, although I hope it isn't lunch already. I don't like losing track of time—I'm missing too much already.

Footsteps scuff to a stop on the balcony. "It's just me," a deep voice rumbles. "Aleks."

I knew the voice even before he said his name. "Sorry, the sun is blinding! Come on down."

There's no sound for a moment, then I hear him trotting down the steps, and I can finally see him away from the glare. Ember and Niko have visited several times over the last couple days, but this garden paradise is getting a wee bit lonely. Which I guess explains my big smile as Aleks steps into the shade with me. He's dressed more casually now—not the scrubs from before, just some extremely well-fitting jeans and a black t-shirt that shows off his trim, muscular form quite nicely.

"Hey," I say. "You came back."

He's standing just under the vine-covered pergola, not getting too close. "I wasn't sure if you'd want me to." He bites his lip, and I knew he was sexy before, even in my hazy state—and then the freaked out one—but that little bit of uncertainty is all kinds of cute. And it reminds me of the part I did like—when he cried about the murdered girl, the one I didn't save, and then he let me wipe away his tears. It takes a strong man to allow a woman he doesn't even know to do that.

I stop the swing and scoot over, patting the bench. "Come have a seat."

His eyes widen a little, but he doesn't hesitate, just slides into the bench-made-for-two. The seat creaks a little, and I remember he's one of *them*—a dragon. Ember told me.

"How are you feeling?" he asks.

"Better with company." I smile. "You gotta push, though." I nudge the ground with my toes, but I can't get the swing to move with his substantial weight.

His answering grin is like the sun, and he pushes

the pavers with his upscale boots. As we swing, he steadies the bench with one hand on the chain and the other on the back. His fingers are just a few inches from my shoulder, and the wild idea of sliding over and cuddling takes hold of my brain. I remember the feel of his hands on my body—I was freaking out, but he was nothing but calm, strong, and gentle. It was nice. Very nice.

I really should apologize—for the freakout—but then we talk at the same time.

"Hey, I'm sorry about—" I say as he blurts out, "I'm sorry I rushed—"

We stop and smile. There's something about him that just feels... *comfortable.* Which is strange because I don't do people that easily. From behind a camera? *Yes.* In real life? Smaller doses are better.

"I'll go first," he says with a tempered smile, "because you don't have anything to apologize for. I, on the other hand, am a complete idiot for trying to rush you into my world." He gives a little shrug. "I can be impatient about some things."

"Yeah?" I give him a flirtatious look, which is really *not* me, but I'm feeling bold in this garden of delights. Plus those pretty gray eyes are reeling me in. "What kinds of things?"

I swear the color of his eyes darkens, and he

cocks his head ever-so-slightly to the side. "Things like bringing beautiful Dragon Spirits into my world."

I grin because *that look*—it's making me feel kind of bubbly and light inside. And *holy hotness,* I need to get this guy on film. Would he model for me? "I'm not so sure I buy all that," I tease.

But his face clouds. "I thought Ember said—"

"Oh, I believe the dragon part," I explain quickly. "I mean, *obviously.* She shifted right in front of me. Not sure about this business with the birth-mark making me a soul mate to a dragon. Not that dragons aren't sexy." I lean forward and whisper, "Niko shifted for me, too. I promised to close my eyes when he shifted back, but I lied."

A flash of *something* crosses his face, but he doesn't find it quite as funny as I thought he might. "You like to peek, do you?"

Oh. So we're playing it like that. "I *am* a photographer. I admire the human body in all its forms." I am *definitely* getting this sexy man to model for me at some point.

"I see." His beautiful gray eyes are *on fire.* "Then it's a good thing I brought you a camera."

The humor drops off my face. "You what?"

He jumps up from the swing and trots back to

the balcony. I shield my eyes, but he disappears again into the glare. A moment later, he's coming back… *with a bulky DSLR camera in his hand.* I can tell it's stupid expensive before he even gets back to the swing. As he sits, I just stare at it, resting in his lap. I haven't touched a camera since that day—the day I put my equipment down and walked away.

I slowly drag my gaze up to meet his. "Why?" My heart's thudding and my head is buzzing. I'm both chastising myself for reacting like a crazy person—it's just a fucking camera—and feeling an irrational fear of touching the thing.

"You don't have to take it if you don't want to." He's peering at me with those sparkling gray eyes. "But before you decide, I want you to know that I get it. I understand completely what it's like to live with a regret that you can never take back, never change, never do fucking anything about but move forward."

He has my entire attention now.

"So, you know I'm pretty old, right?" His smile is crooked, but I know he's not joking.

"Like two hundred years?" Ember told me about the dragons being driven out of their original lair in Greece. How some of the ones that live now in Niko's castle, somewhere here in the Thousand

Islands, are from that time, including Aleks. Because apparently, dragons have super long lives.

Aleks's smile turns mischevious. "Two hundred and nineteen." Then he gets serious. "Niko and I are cousins, but we were born in the same year. Twenty years before our home lair was attacked and burned to the ground. Did Ember tell you why we escaped? Why we didn't perish like all our friends and family?"

I just shake my head, eyes wide.

"Because we were young and stupid and thought that a soul mate was some kind of prison we didn't want to get trapped in." He shakes his head. "Did I mention stupid? I've spent the last two hundred years doing nothing but desperately searching for my soul mate."

I lean a little away because I hadn't thought of it that way—the soul mate thing seemed silly or maybe romantic but not a *desperate* thing. I mean, Ember explained their predicament—that's why she's intent on making a dragon baby—but I hadn't thought of it from the dragon's perspective. From the viewpoint of the hot, flirtatious, sweet man sharing my swing.

His expression locks down. "So, while my family and friends burned to death, I was fucking my way across Europe." He smiles, but it's bitter. "Barmaids and farmers' daughters. Noble women and nuns—more than one nun. Let me tell you, nunneries are a *hotbed* of action for the right young sheepherder come to tend sheep."

I smile despite the ache in my heart for this man. "Sounds like you had fun."

"Yes, I did." Small lines form at the corners of his eyes, but it's not a smile. More like pain. "And if I hadn't been off romancing the continent, I would have died like everyone else. So I shouldn't regret it, right? I mean, that's crazy. And yet, I do. Every day."

I nod. Fervently. "Because maybe you could have done something."

"Right?" And there's a deeply buried anger starting to surface. "Surely, Aleksandr Drayce Ardunur Blackscale, twenty-year-old expert seducer of nuns, could have done *something* to stop a massive magical attack that wiped out his people and everyone he loved."

I want to say something, but the words are tangled in my throat.

He keeps going. *"Surely,* I could have done some-thing better than literally fuck around." His anger —at himself, clear as day—seems to peak. He drops his gaze to the camera he's cradling in his lap. "But I *did* do something," he says softly. Then he looks up, and those eyes of his are sparkling with unshed tears. "I survived."

I want to touch him—I want to hold his cheek again and brush away his tears—but it feels awkward now. So I just say, "If you hadn't survived, there would be nothing left." And it punches me right in the gut. I suddenly know why Ember is making babies with her hot dragon lover. Because I know my sister—the instant she heard this story, she would be all-in on racing to the rescue in any way she could.

"Everything we've done since that day," he continues, "was to survive. To keep going. To make things *better* in any way we could. For us, collectively, that means finding our soul mates. Keeping the species going. For me, personally, it was keeping my cousin, my brother-dragon, Niko from falling into a pit of despair. Because that guy…" He shakes his head. "I love him, but he carries the burden of that day even more than me. I can't tell you how glad I am that he found your sister."

My heart swells with that. Because as much as Ember and I might fight—or really just argue like sisters do—I want everything wonderful in the world for her. And I wasn't sold on this soul mate business. The lingering doubt that maybe it was all a story, maybe Niko was just insanely hot in bed, or something worse like he was conning her into making dragon babies... but the love in Aleks's eyes for his brother dragon is *real*.

"I guess she really is his soul mate." The idea still seems strange. I've had plenty of boyfriends—some sweet, some outright bastards who cheated on me—and I would have sworn that I loved each and every one of them. But soul mate? It doesn't make sense there could only be one person in the whole world you were meant to love.

"You have a soul mate, too," he says quietly, playing with the strap of the camera he's brought for me. "I don't know who he is..." He looks up. "But I'm already jealous of him."

I can't help the smile—my whole body is warming up, and it's not the sun. I nod to the camera. "Is that why you're bringing me presents?"

His smile is back. "Ember told me about the awards you've won. That you've been behind a camera most of your life. You can't let what's happened stop you from doing what you're meant to do." He holds it out to me.

I'm surprised how easy it is for me to take it.

Like everything seems *easy* with Aleks. Although that's not quite right—everything is *real* with him. And that makes it easy. There's no pretending. No hiding. Just an open heart. I've met a lot of people in the world—on shoots, on the road, reporting with Ember—and people like him are vanishingly rare.

I look the camera over. Top of the line. I haven't even seen this model yet. It's a standard DSLR—Digital Single Lens Reflex—but the bottom plate says it has 50 Megapixel full-frame CMOS sensor, really precise autofocus tracking, and a dedicated processor for all that digital speed. Very nice.

I peer through the viewfinder at the handsome man who I barely know but who's managed to put a camera back in my hands when I thought that might never happen. I snap his picture before he can get wise to what I'm doing.

"Wait," he protests. "Did you just—"

I grin and snap another one of his slightly alarmed expression. "What did you think I would do?"

"Flowers." He dips his head to chastise me with those beautiful eyes. "I expected you to take pictures of flowers."

I zoom and get that shot I wanted of just his

eyes. Then I lower the camera just as an idea crashes through my brain. *Ohhh.* "Aleks," I say, my heart speeding up again. "Will you model for me?"

"What?" He shakes his head, fast and panicky. "I'm not a—"

"As a dragon." I hold his startled gaze—I'm serious about this.

He shakes his head like he should have known better, then he rises up from the swing. I'm on my feet in an instant.

"I need more room," he says with a smirk for the pergola over our heads.

"By the fountain." I'm breathless. I'm not sure why this is so exciting—*fuck*, yes, I do. He's a *dragon*. And I'm about to take the world's first pictures of one. Maybe. I don't know, someone must have taken pictures before, but they've remained hidden because of course—Aleks's people are hunted. So these are just for me. *Private.* Maybe that's what's got my heart fluttering as he steps backward, tipping his head for me to follow. I stumble after, the hot pavers burning my feet, and I couldn't care less. Although I do step onto the grass once we reach the fountain.

"You ready?" he asks, a grin playing across his face.

"Oh, yes." I sight him through the viewfinder

and quickly snap a couple because he's just gorgeous even in human form. Then from one snap to the next, he shifts. I stumble back reflexively because he suddenly fills the whole frame. I crouch and snap, camera glued to my face, my view flicking from a hasty glance at the ground so I don't trip as I move and the viewfinder taking in his beautiful black dragon form. The water fountain is blocked from view. His scales shine metallic in the sun. His four legs (arms?) have feet (hands?) with talons like the cruelest of daggers. His head is ridged, his eyes still gray, and his long, serpentine neck is flexing for me. *Posing.* I grin as I shoot, moving and desperately trying to capture the majesty of his beast form. I back up nearly to the pergola for a wider view, and he unfolds his wings, spreading them for me to capture every bony ridge, every scaly part, even the feathers that extend at the tips. He's magnificent, and my heart sings as I snap it all.

Then suddenly, he shifts again, and I'm shooting him naked. I'm startled... *then greedy.* Zooming in, I capture his broad shoulders, muscular chest, legs built like they're made of iron bands, and between... an erection that makes my heart skip a beat. I stop when he bends down to scoop his clothes off the ground and holds them in front of his body, protesting with an outstretched hand.

"Tell me you did not…"

I lower the camera and smile.

"Oh, *fuck me.*" He hastily pulls on his pants and shirt, and I'm not even shy about enjoying the view. When he's done, he storms over with delicious menace on his face. "Give it to me."

"What?" But I hold the camera away.

He reaches for it, but I skitter backward, keeping it out of his reach. "Are you kidding me —" he protests, chasing after me, and I give a small shriek as I barely slip out of his grasp and stumble around the swing. The big wooden bench is between us now but only momentarily as he feints and then pulls the swing *over his head,* and suddenly, there's no space between us. He's got one hand clamped around my wrist—the one holding the camera—and the other goes around my waist, holding *me,* so I don't slip away. "I need you to delete those pictures." His voice is a little hoarse.

I dare him with my eyes.

His eyes are a gray storm growing darker.

I swear he's going to kiss me—I *want* him to— then he releases me and steps back.

"You can keep them." It's some promise I don't understand.

But the kiss that failed to happen stabs a little disappointment through me. "Aleks, I'm sorry—"

"It's okay." He tucks in his shirt and takes another step back. But then he levels a *full-of-promise* look at me, the sexy kind. The kind that says that kiss is *on hold* not *forgotten*. "Maybe you'll enjoy looking at them when you're alone."

A full-body flush leaves me speechless for a moment—just long enough for him to turn and stride toward the balcony, scooping up his abandoned shoes along the way. Before I can think of what to say to get him to stay... he's gone.

I lift the camera and flip through the pictures.

Oh yes. I definitely need to find alone time with these.

Then I look toward the tiny cottage that's been my home for days—weeks, really—and wonder...

If he wants me thinking of him that way, why did he run away?

FIVE

Aleksandr

I AM SO FUCKED.

Not literally… but that's an idea. Maybe if I go to the party downstairs, I can find some pretty young thing, bring her up to my room, and spend the night making her scream my name. Maybe then I'll forget about Ms. Cinder Dubois. Only I don't think it will work. And the mere thought is making me nauseous. Yet, I'm dutifully putting on my party clothes—tailored pants, trim black silk shirt, practically a uniform for dragons on the hunt.

I stare at the mirror as I button my sleeves.

I should have just kissed her. I had Cinder in my arms this morning. She was flirting with me from the moment I arrived. She *wanted* me to kiss her. You don't spend two hundred years romancing human women to that first kiss without knowing when it's right. *It was right.* I blinked. I drew back.

I didn't want to know.

If I'd kissed her, the mystery would have been gone. I'd *know* she wasn't my soul mate. Then there would be no more flirtation. No more heartfelt confessions. None of that would be appropriate. And her mate—whoever he ended up being— would *not* appreciate me planting her in that swing and driving my cock into her until she came, multiple times, as I've been fantasizing about non-stop. It's an unwritten, but ironclad, rule of the lair: once you know, let her go. There's a one-night rule. After all, that first kiss can be pretty damn hot. If she's into you, and you're already grinding her up against a wall, no one will hold one night against you. But that's it. *Catch and release.* If she's not yours, and you do anything but pack her up and send her to the next dragon when the morning comes, her mate—when he finds out—will come for your head. And his brothers will help. And you'll deserve it. Because only a fucking asshole would do that. Only once a woman's been through the entire lair—and the other three as well—only once it's known that she's *not* Dragon Spirited, are you allowed to keep her. And by then, most women have grown tired of the endless hookups, just as most dragons do, and they drift away.

One night. That's the most I could have with Cinder. And if I'd kissed her under the damn pergola, I wouldn't have even had that. My only real job here is to prepare her for the gauntlet. I didn't think she was ready, but the way she was flirting with me today... I can't stop that either.

And it's eating me alive. Already.

I'm still staring at my haunted face in the mirror when my phone buzzes.

Niko. I pick it up. "What?"

"Where are you? I thought you were coming down." I can hear the murmur of voices in the background. He's downstairs at the party, wondering where the fuck I am.

"On my way." I hang up. To my stupidly-in-love-already mug in the mirror, I say, "You go down there. You find the hottest girl. And you keep her up all night. That's what you do. That's how you get past this." My reflection isn't buying any of it.

I force myself to march out of my apartment.

The party's in full swing. Music floats up through the central stairs and bounces down the hallways. I see at least two dragons disappearing into the party rooms—not their apartments, but the small hotel-type rooms we built near the main hall. Sometimes, they'll head up even before the first kiss. It's kind of awkward to do that in public. Besides, the first kiss isn't always a True Kiss—the kind that comes with a baring of souls. That's part of the one-night rule because it can take a few orgasms before a woman opens her heart to you. I almost wish it had been that way with Cinder—that I'd have to properly seduce her to get her to open up. That's part of my fantasy, too. That we've met for the first time at a party. That she's coy about that wound she's carrying around, wishing she'd done more to save that little girl. And then I'd coax it out of her, one nibble at a time. One orgasm at a time. And only at the end—only when I'd thoroughly pleasured her—would she kiss me with her entire heart.

But that's not how Cinder works. I can tell already—the first kiss, and I'd know.

Fuck.

I've reached the bottom of the stairs. Niko raises his glass to me from across the room. Ember's at his side, looking amazing in a short black dress that shows off her curves. The same curves—the same face, almost—that Cinder has. It's killing me, so I veer off and head for the front room. Constantine is there, bringing drinks to a group of women —all young and beautiful. He's one of our main recruiters, so he's probably the quickest shot at getting this done.

"Champagne for Liza," Constantine says, handing her a flute. "Red wine for Isabelle. And you two ladies wanted white, correct? I'll be right back."

I lift my chin to him as I join their group. "I'll give you a hand."

He lifts an eyebrow but nods. I fall in step with him to head to the bar.

"I thought you had a patient to attend to," he says quietly. He gives the bartender the order for the white wines. We have a limit on how much alcohol each potential mate gets before she's "brought inside," i.e., sworn to secrecy and shown what we are. Drunk kisses are sloppy, dubious consent, and most importantly, not True Kisses. But a glass of wine or two is invaluable for getting everyone warmed up.

I order a scotch.

"I've got a problem," I say to Constantine, "and I need your help." I give an appraising look back to the group of four. Two blondes, a red-head, and a dark-haired girl who looks nothing like Cinder. Any of them will do.

He peers at the women. "I thought your problem was out at the cottage."

"She is." The bartender delivers my scotch first, and I knock it back.

Constantine's eyes narrow. "Then why are you here?"

"Because she's not." I'm surprised he hasn't gotten the memo from Niko. The one that says it's *Get Aleks Laid Night.* Constantine must have just arrived.

He lifts an eyebrow and accepts the two wine glasses from the bartender, but he doesn't make a move to leave the bar. "We really need that intel, Aleks."

"She doesn't remember anything."

He looks baffled. "Isn't that why you're—"

"I just *can't*, okay?" I snap.

"What the... Oh, shit. *Really?*" He's stunned.

I just nod. Falling in love—or even just rolling out your heart—even before the first kiss is a rookie move. I'm no rookie—I haven't been for a long damn time. Neither is Constantine. He's the consummate pro, seducing women in the city then bringing them up to the lair. Sometimes in groups, like the ones here tonight.

"I just need someone for the night." It feels dirty to say it, and not in a good way. "Just to take the edge off."

Constantine double taps the bar. "Another scotch for my brother."

That might actually help. I give him a tight smile.

"I'm still worried about this witch," he says as we wait for my drink.

"It's been more than two weeks," I offer. The effects of the first drink are hitting my bloodstream, a little liquid calm to numb the pain. "Nothing's happened. They haven't come for Cinder. They haven't found the lair. Maybe we're in the clear."

"What about this Julia woman, the one Cinder mentioned?" Constantine frowns. "She could be a soul mate."

"She could be a fever dream." My drink arrives, and I knock that back too, breathing through the fumes. "Cinder doesn't remember *anything.* And as long as that's true, we're just flying blind. We can't go back for this Julia person even if we wanted to."

"We could go after the witch."

I lean back. "You're really concerned about her. Even though she saved us."

"She's a risk to every one of us."

I guess he's not wrong about that. "I'll talk to Niko about it. *In the morning.*" I give another glance at the group of four women. Constantine's a pro in every way—I'm sure they're all fiery and spirited, even if they're not, in the end, Dragon Spirits. They're beautiful on the outside, that's for sure. My body should have no problem responding once I have them undressed and under me. If not, there's always more scotch—the limits on alcohol are for the women, not the dragons.

"What flavor do you like tonight?" Constantine asks, handing me one of the white wines.

"Whichever's most ready." It's callous by any standard.

"You sure about this?" He's frowning at me as we weave our way back to the group. And he's not wrong to worry, either. Any dragon's need to get laid should always take a back seat to taking the utmost care with a potential mate. The only way she'll get through the entire lair is if each dragon does his part in making it worth her while.

"I'm okay to do this. Promise." I lean close, so

only he can hear. "Which one is looking for a wild night? Because I've got some energy to burn."

"All right, then." He straightens and puts on a smile for the four women. "Ladies, this is my cousin, Aleks! Eliana, my love, Aleks needs your dancing expertise. Perhaps you can show him some moves, so he stops embarrassing the rest of us."

I hand Eliana her white wine and give her my best smile. "I'd love to see what you can do." She's one of the blondes, and her body's off the charts—long, lean, muscular legs showing through a thigh-high slit in her flame-red dress; pert, high breasts; and most important, hungry eyes.

Her smile is pure heat. She sips at the wine and gives me her hand. I clasp it, and without a word, she's dragging me out of the front room. I wonder if Constantine's already had her up in the rooms because she's heading straight for the stairs. Which is a relief, honestly. Some hard-charging sex is just the thing I need, all the better if there's no romance at all involved.

As we head up the stairs, the noise of the party dims a little. Eliana looks me over. "Are you really Constantine's cousin?"

I'm not sure what he's told her, so I go with the

truth. "We come from the same small community in the Greek Isles. Everyone's a cousin there." It's practically true. Back before preserving the species was our primary concern, bringing women in from the "outside" was still key to keeping the genetic diversity of the lair robust. We didn't know about that then— science has progressed a lot in two hundred years— but we knew that each new mating brought freshness to the sprawling, interconnected families of the lair.

She smirks. "Kissing cousins?"

"Not exactly." She's definitely not read-in yet— Constantine may have slept with her, but he hasn't revealed himself. And that won't be happening tonight with me, either. "Let's try this one," I say, indicating the closest party room. I pull her clasped hand toward the door. There's a simple code for knowing if it's occupied—the button on the handle is vertical (for taken) or horizontal (for unoccupied). This one's empty. I knock for show, then swing the door open.

I've barely got the door closed before her hands are circling my waist, and she's shoving me back against the door. "Your cousin kept up with me all night long." She licks her lips as she peers up at me. "Do you think you can handle me?"

"We're about to find out." I fist my hand in her

hair and tip her head back, ready to start a feast that will hopefully jump-start my cock—it's MIA so-far—when my phone buzzes in my pocket. *"Fuck,"* I breathe on her neck, where I was about to take a bite.

"Leave it." She grinds her body against mine, practically climbing me.

"I need to…" I gently extricate myself from her clutches. Niko wouldn't be messaging me if it weren't important. And no one else fucking texts on party night.

It's from Cinder. *What the*—how the hell did she get my number? "I've gotta take this—" I say as I tap open the message. It's a picture. *Of my cock.* *"Holy shit."* I scramble to keep Eliana from seeing the text while quickly scanning the rest. I'M ENJOYING YOUR PICTURES, it says, then there's a video with a frozen image of Cinder's body in just her underwear, from her breasts to her sweet sex. *Holy fuck.* My cock springs to attention.

"What is it?" Eliana's trying to peer at the text.

I quickly turn off my phone. "An emergency." *Shit.* What do I do? But my cock is already making plans. "I have to go. I'm sorry."

"What kind of emergency?" Eliana's frown is tinged with anger.

I'm stuffing my phone in my pocket and nudging her away from the door, so I can leave. I grab her shoulders and kiss her forehead as I shuffle her back just enough. "I'm so sorry," I repeat. "Tell Constantine I had to go take care of something. He'll find someone to keep you company. Promise." I've got the door open, so I release her and literally run down the hall. There's a balcony off an office at the end, so I head for that. I'm through the office and flinging open the balcony doors before I remember I haven't watched the video.

I stop, dig out my phone, and tap it to play. There's no sound—no, there are no *words;* I can hear Cinder sigh, and it makes my cock ache. She's holding the phone so it just shows her bra and panties—delicate, pink lace barely hiding her hardened nipples and the mound of softness between her legs. Her hand appears in the video, fingers tracing a circle around her breast then trailing down her sweet belly and sliding into the panties.

The video stops there.

Holy fuck. I stuff the phone in my pocket, shift into my dragon form, barely remember to snag my clothes, then unfold my wings and leap from the balcony. The air is warm, the night dark, and I'm in a heedless, maniacal rush to get to her. I don't fucking care that we'll only have tonight. I'll kiss her first to make that very clear—to dash that hope right away. Then I will make love to her *all* night long. I just *need* her in a way I haven't needed anything in a long time. And she wants it—she's practically stamped *mine* across my cock with that zoomed-in image. *Fuck.* I'm so hard for her, it's draining the sense out of my head, and I almost miss the honeymooner's cottage island. I land outside by the fountain. Light spills out of her room between the slats in the blinds. I shift and grab my pants, trying to button around my painfully erect cock. It's almost impossible, but I manage it. I leave the shirt behind and storm up the stairs. When I yank open the door, I have to shove aside the blinds, but when I do, she's waiting for me, a smirk on her face, lying on her side, head propped on her hand, those pink panties and bra still on her body.

Not for long.

"You got my text?" she says innocently.

I just growl and stride fast across the room. Her eyes go a little wide as I climb onto the bed and cover her with my body, pressing her back into the pillows, holding her wrists over her head. I'm so full of *need*, I barely know where to start. I lower my head to her neck and bury my teeth in her, just hard enough to let her know I'm *serious* about making her scream. She gasps and arches into me. Her small whimper has me letting go of the bite, tasting her before I whisper, "Did you do it?"

"Do what?" *Oh,* the need in her voice. My cock is begging for release from my pants.

"Did you pleasure yourself while looking at my cock?" I'm nibbling at her ear as I say it.

She sucks air between her teeth. "I thought the real thing might be better."

Fuck. Me. "I guarantee you, it will."

I pull back and look at her hooded eyes, her parted lips, and I've never seen anything so beautiful and so primally feminine.

"Are you going to hold me down while you ravish me?" she asks. The smirk playing across her lips says she would like that very much. But it makes me realize I've got her pinned—my hands locked around her wrists, holding them above her head, my body, including my painfully erect cock, pressing her into the bed.

I release her hands and try to rein myself in. Just a little. Just enough to do this right. I hold myself off her body, just enough to take off the weight, then I caress her mussed hair back from her face and gaze into those beautiful amber-green eyes.

"I'm going to ravish you five different ways, Cinder Dubois."

Her eyes light up with that.

"But first…" My heart leaps into my throat. "But *first…*" I lean in because I need to know. I need that kiss to tell me she's *not* mine, and that I need to make the most of tonight. I nuzzle her cheek and whisper into her ear, "I need to know if you want this as much as I do." That should do it— that should open her up to giving me a True Kiss.

I barely move to kiss her before she grabs the back of my neck and pulls me in. Her lips are hungry for mine. Her tongue plunges deep, ravishing *me* with her need. I press into the kiss, my heart wildly thudding, my hands bunching in her hair and grabbing at the bed, this kiss suddenly consuming me. There's nothing left in the universe, just her mouth against mine, her tongue married to mine, and a frantic panting as we breathe through something much closer to sex than kissing. Closer to lovemaking than simple tasting. We are *joined* by this kiss, and as my heart threatens to beat its way out of my chest, I realize…

She's the one.

I gasp and pull back, staring wide-eyed at her under me. Her lips are swollen from our kiss. Her eyes are nearly closed in pleasure. She lazily gazes up at me. "And that's just the start?" she asks, thickly.

Holy fuck. "You're my…" The words catch in my throat.

"I'm what?" She blinks, coming out of the haze. Does she know? Can she feel it?

There's a connection seared into me, spearing straight through my body, connecting my soul to hers. I've never been more sure of something in all my life.

Soul mate. "You're the most amazing woman I've ever known." Simple truth.

She grins. "I'm half-naked, Aleks. You don't need to flatter me into bed. Already here."

I just shake my head, dazedly, then slowly sink to the bed next to her. "I want you so badly." I caress her cheek. Truer words were never spoken. *But she doesn't know.* That she's my soul mate. That we're two halves of the same dragon spirit. That I'm destined to be hers, she's mine, and there will never be another for either of us. I can tell by the casual flirtation in her eyes… whereas I feel like I'm being melted by the sun.

"I mean… *yes.*" She smiles wider. "Did I not make that clear with the video? Yes, Aleks, my personal hot dragon attendant, I want your cock. Badly."

Oh, fuck me. I can't make love to her like this— casually—not until she knows. Not until she understands the full ramifications of what happens when you make love to your soul mate. Because it can happen in the middle of an orgasm. It can happen with a simple word. She might not start out being in love with me but by the end of the night—well, it's not my prowess in bed that will win her heart. It's the fact that she already owns mine. That she opens her heart without question—she's already done it with me before. We *would* be mated by the end of the night, and that's not something you can spring on someone without warning.

I run my hand into her hair and kiss her again, gently. It's soft and slow, but the same sense of connection zings through me. I've never felt something like that before—not in two hundred years. And not because I didn't want to. This is something completely new.

I pull back from the kiss and press my forehead to hers, closing my eyes. "God, I love that."

She laughs a little. "Kissing?"

I look deep into her eyes. "Kissing *you*. Being with you. Talking to you. I sat by your bedside for two weeks just to *look* at you. Just to be there when you woke up."

She frowns a little. "Did I wake up a lot? I don't remember."

I smile. "No, you never did remember me. It was like meeting you for the first time, a hundred times."

She touches my face with her fingertips, trailing them across my cheek. "You're so... different. There's something about you that's just... I don't know. How did I luck into having you take care of me?"

She's so close. Maybe, with another kiss, she'll *feel* it like I do. "It's not luck." Then I press her into the pillow with my kiss, hungry and open, unabashed in my need for her. It's the frantic kind of kiss that could quickly escalate into sex. I growl with the need to have her right fucking now. But I can't—*I won't*—so I finish the kiss and force myself to pry my body off hers.

"Oh, God, don't tell me you're a tease," she pants. "You're killing me." She's grabbing at my face to bring me back.

I press her hand to my cheek then pull it away. *"Cinder."* My breathing is ragged too. I kiss the inside of her wrist, right over her birthmark. "I'm falling for you. So hard."

Conflict torments her face. She's not in love with me, not yet—or she's unwilling to say it. And she hasn't felt the connection either—or that would change everything. She's just squirming under me and wondering why I won't give her what she's so plainly asking for.

"It's okay—" I start.

"No, it's not." She bites her lip. "I *really* like you, Aleks. I mean, you're amazingly sweet and hot. You're exactly the kind of man I *would* love, if I'd known you for more than a few days…"

"You don't have to—" I try again.

"No." She's determined now, bringing our hands down to clasp on her chest and giving me a serious look. "It's not fair. To you. And you deserve better than that." Her teeth rake over her lower lip again. "You're just ahead of me, that's all. You were *awake* these last couple weeks. If only I could remember some of it…" She frowns, hard, and drops her gaze like she's trying to summon all those times when she was half confused, half asleep.

"There's no rush," I breathe, relieved she doesn't want to push it. We need time to talk about all of it before we take that leap. "We can just… kiss. For now. I can make that worth your time." I reach for her, planning to draw her back into another hot-as-hell kiss.

She gasps. But I haven't touched her.

She meets my gaze, and the horror on her face stops me cold. *"I remember."*

SIX

Cinder

I THOUGHT THE *COTTAGE* WAS BEAUTIFUL—EMBER'S boyfriend lives in a literal *castle*.

Aleks had whisked me out of bed, we threw on clothes, and then he hurried me off the little island retreat where I've been staying for weeks. A motorboat ride across dark, glassy water brought us to this lit-up, fairytale castle on another of the Thousand Islands. And if the outside was like a storybook, the inside was pure decadence. Stained-glass dome in the main hall. Sweeping marble staircases. Chandeliers and hors d'oeuvres and beautiful people drinking and flirting. Aleks hurried me upstairs to an opulent office lined with bookcases, a huge desk, and windows open to the nighttime sky. Niko, Ember, and another beautiful man they introduced as Constantine quickly joined us. Are all dragons gorgeous? I think they must be.

Now I'm folded up in the corner of the leather couch, chewing at my thumbnail.

"Did the witch bring you to the Vardigah?" Constantine demands.

"The Vardigah?" I ask.

"The dark elves," Ember supplies.

"I don't think so." It's still all so fuzzy.

"What did they do to you? Do you remember?" Niko asks.

"Bad things." I suck in a breath, trying to be brave, but the memories are slippery.

"What about Julia?" Constantine asks. "Can you remember her now?" He flicks a look to Niko.

"I... think so?" I'm trying to put all the pieces together, honestly. It's just a mess inside my head.

"Okay, back up," Aleks says, but he's not talking to me. He's physically backing up everyone who's crowded around my couch, barraging me with questions. "Give her some space. And half a second to sort this out before you interrogate the shit out of her, okay?"

They all talk at once, but not to me—Aleks is my shield, and I want to kiss him for it. Actually, I want to go back to our island retreat and make mad sexy love to him. Kissing him was like nothing I've felt before—it was so pure, so sweet, and yet, at the same time, so hot I was ready to strap him to the bed and have my way with him. And that was just the kiss—what would riding the man's cock be like? It's a beautiful cock, thick and long with a perfectly shaped head that looks positively delicious. I had plenty of time to admire it on my phone, once I got the pictures transferred. But we didn't get to the cock-admiration stage before my memories came flooding back. It's like the kiss opened up something inside me—a vault that was holding all my missing time, and now I'm having to sort the memories out, one by one, and put them back in order. Or make some sense of them. And that's hard to do with everyone shouting and losing their damn minds.

I know this is important—I'm doing my best. But I'd be lost without Aleks to run interference right now. I close my eyes, rub my temples, and try to *focus.*

I knew what the Vardigah looked like even before my memories came back—that alien in my bedroom was one of them. But now I have a thousand reasons to loathe and fear them as much as Aleks's people do. *The Vardigah tortured me.* My mind is still giving me some kind of buffer against that. I know I'm not sensing the full horror of what they did. But I have clear memories of being strapped to a chair, held in place by a dozen pincher-type appendages that came from beneath, like being wrapped up in the legs of an overturned beetle. The pain didn't come from the restraints—it came from the psychic probe they used on my mind. I don't know what else to call the crystal wand they pointed at my temple. But when they did, a blinding pain felt like it was tearing me apart—not physically, but *my mind.* I don't think they were trying to kill me. In fact, I distinctly remember them freaking out when one session was so horrible that I blacked out. When I came to, they were running frantically around the room, blasting my body with electric magic, forcing air into my lungs with a horrible tube down my throat. They settled down again when they saw I was awake. Then they went right back to zapping my mind with their magic. Fucking *assholes* were trying to do something. Experimenting on me. But for what? It wasn't like they asked me questions. They never spoke to me at all.

I was a lab rat.

And so was Julia.

I remember her now, in the next cell over. I only saw her once, when the Vardigah came for her at the same time they were returning me to my cell. But we could talk through the vents that brought fresh air to our cells, connecting us through their magic glowing walls. She'd been there for a week. She warned me when they first came for me what lay in store. We cried together. And as I'm piecing all this together, I'm realizing… *she's still there.* And she's been there for two weeks. Guilt stabs me so hard I cave over, clutching my stomach. *I didn't know.* I couldn't remember—my mind was too shattered by what had happened. I don't know why I can remember now. Maybe kissing Aleks was just the right healing to let that happen. I don't know. But I need to *do something* about Julia.

Aleks notices I'm hunched over. He leaves the bickering group and hurries to kneel by the couch. "You okay?"

I breathe through the sickness in my belly. "Aleks, we need to go back for Julia."

The chatter comes to a halt. "That's what I'm talking about," Constantine says, approval in his voice.

Ember's frowning my direction.

Niko's likewise concerned. "You remember her now?"

I nod. "She was in the cell next to me. The Vardigah tortured us both."

Aleks is up off the floor in an instant, climbing on the couch with me, putting an arm around my shoulders. His fist is clenched and pressing into his knee. *"Fucking bastards,"* he hisses through his teeth. He looks like he wants to murder something. "You don't have to talk about this—"

I put a hand to his cheek. "It's okay. *I'm* okay. And I do." I lay my hand on his clenched fist to coax it open. He laces his fingers with mine. The look of pain on his face will undo me, so I turn to the rest of the group to explain. "It was some kind of mental torture. They pressed a magic wand to our heads and scrambled what was inside. I don't know why."

Constantine's frowning and stroking his chin. "The witch who was with you when we arrived— was that what she was doing to you? Some kind of magical torture?" He flicks a look to Niko, who's also highly interested in that question.

"No," I say, reflexively. "Although… I don't really remember the rescue." I glance at Aleks.

"You were out, my love." He strokes my hair, and there's an awkward moment while everyone doesn't know what to say. Because Aleks is suddenly *out there* with kind of, maybe, totally being in love with me. He doesn't seem to care, *at all*, what anyone else thinks about that. It makes me feel warm and gushy inside.

I squeeze his hand. "Okay, so I don't know what Alice was doing when you arrived, but she wouldn't have hurt me. She was trying to help us."

"Hang on," Nikos says. *"Alice?* You know the witch?"

"Red hair?" I say. "Young. Super cute?"

"That's the one," Ember offers.

"So, she was helping you?" Constantine's frown is growing more confused.

"Definitely." This much I'm sure of. "She'd come in after the torture sessions. While the guard was there, she'd keep up the act, all business. I think she was supposed to check to see if whatever they were doing to us actually worked. She never explained that part. But instead, she'd do this healing magic thing." I demonstrate by putting my palm to my forehead. "Like this. And it would help, a little. At least with the pain and the confusion."

Niko and Constantine are having a silent exchange about that. I'm not sure who's convincing who of what.

"Oh!" I add. "And she helped me send a message out to Ember."

"Wait, *the video?*" Ember's eyebrows hike up. "I thought you just texted that to me."

I shrug. "I don't know where the Vardigah live, but they do *not* have cell reception."

Niko gives a hand gesture that says *See?* to Constantine. "You can't text from a different dimension."

Constantine seems to concede the obvious there.

I frown as I realize... "Alice must still have my phone. She never gave it back. Which is weird because I had to show her how to send the text. Like she didn't know how phones worked. But she said she could get to "earth" to send it for me."

Constantine scowls. "So she comes back through the portal in Ireland. Probably to use the Gift. Maybe it doesn't work in the Vardigah realm."

"Maybe." Niko looks to me. "But why would Alice try to help you recover and maybe help us escape if she was the one who brought you there in the first place?"

"Wait, what?" I lean back. "Alice wouldn't do that."

Niko and Constantine share a skeptical look. Niko explains, "Witches, at least in the past, used the Gift to find the soul mates of dragons. And mated dragons are dangerous to the Vardigah. *And* the Vardigah were conducting some kind of magical experiment on you. Those have to be connected."

I slump a little on the couch, but I don't know what to say to that. And this soul mate business still freaks me out. What does that mean for Aleks? He's already said he's falling in love with me, but what if he's not my soul mate?

I'm silent just a little too long because Aleks says, "Okay, that's enough interrogation for tonight."

"We need some kind of plan," Constantine protests.

I agree. "We need to go back and get Julia." My stomach is still in knots.

Aleks dips his head. "We don't have a good way to do that."

"Why not?" I mean, they came to get *me*... but then nobody's talked about that. I feel like everyone has been super protective around me—the focus has been on my recovery and getting my memories back, which is fine, but that means I'm still out of the loop on a lot. And part of that protection detail has been Aleks.

Just as he's about to answer me, the door of the office swings open. "Niko!" gasps a man gripping the frame of the door, a wild look in his eyes. "Come quick. We need you in the front room."

"What's the matter?" Niko demands as he heads toward the door.

"Yiannis just… dropped dead." The man is still breathing hard.

"What?" Constantine strides after Niko, who's reached the door.

"We don't know what happened," the man says, more panic leaking into his voice. "He just collapsed."

Niko looks to Ember before he leaves. "I'll be back."

She nods. Aleks is already on his feet, alarmed, but he seems torn about leaving my side. He's still grasping my hand.

"Go on," I say to him. "Go help Niko."

He gives me a soft look, a quick kiss on the cheek, then he dashes after his friends.

I don't know what is happening downstairs, but I'm unlikely to be able to help. And I need a moment to talk to my sister, anyway. She seems to feel the same because she comes to sit on the couch, taking Aleks's place.

"How are you really doing?" she asks. She means the torture.

I shrug. "I'm okay. It's weird. It's like... I remember what happened, but I don't really *feel* it. Does that make sense?"

She nods and takes hold of my hand. "Sounds like it's better this way. I almost wish you didn't remember any of it, now. I'm sorry I dragged you into this dragon business. You don't need to be involved in all this."

I tip my head. "I'm involved whether we like it or not. And it's not *all* bad." I waggle my eyebrows.

Ember chirps a laugh and lets go of my hand. "Okay, *spill.* Just exactly how deeply is Aleks in love with you?"

I turn to face her more fully. "Enough that I need a *lot* more information. Aleks is one fine, fine man. I mean, this castle is *filled* with hot men, but he's different. I really like him, and I'd really like to jump that body of his. But what if he's not "the one?" I mean, I don't know if I even believe this soul mate business." Somehow that seems crazier than magic shape-shifting dragons, witches, and torturous, evil elves. Then again, those things don't impact who I can spend my life with, so maybe it's just personal.

"The soul mate thing is *totally* real," she insists. "And trust me, you want to find your soul mate because everything is better that way. The sex is *insane,* but it's more than that. It's a connection."

"But I feel connected to Aleks." Even if I'm not yet to the *I love you* stage… it's making me kind of panicky to think that I might have to leave him to go on a quest for some other sexy dragon. "I mean, how do you know?"

She narrows her eyes. "Wait, have you guys already done the deed?"

"No, we've just kissed." This whole memory recall thing ruined all my plans in that regard.

"Like a *real* kiss?" She raises her eyebrows. When I nod, she adds, "The dragons call it a True Kiss. It's one where, if they're your soul mate, you can feel that connection. I didn't know what it was at first, but it was definitely there. I think the dragons feel it stronger."

I frown. "I can't say I had any earth-shattering revelation when I kissed Aleks. Other than the very sincere conviction that I wanted to shackle him to my bed and ravish his body."

She smirks. "Well, that's part of it." Then the

smirk falls away. "Wait, is that when you got your memories back?"

"Well, yeah, now that you put it that way." And it did feel like kissing Aleks healed something inside me—I just thought it was the natural thing that happens when you care about someone. Now, I'm lost.

"Talk to him," she says, her expression suddenly serious. "You need to know, Cinder. Before you take things any further."

I frown. "Okay, you're freaking me out. Why?"

Ember grimaces. "I should have told you this sooner. I didn't think it would come up so quick. But I don't know why I thought that—dragon men are ridiculously hot."

"I mean *yes, obviously,* but what are you talking about?" The clench in my stomach is like a permanent fixture now.

"I'm a dragon now, right? Because I'm mated to Niko. Well, that transition happened *when* we mated—like literally *in the act.* It was part of the deal."

"So when—*I mean if*—I decide to mate with a sexy dragon man who's my soul mate, I'm going to turn into a dragon. Got it." This whole thing is just nuts, but I understand that part.

"Yes, but it's not really a decision so much as… two very specific actions."

"Okay." She's got my full attention now. Because I don't want to randomly turn into a dragon without *choosing* that. What the fuck?

"You have to fall in love. And you have to make love. Then… poof, you're a dragon. And by *poof* I mean your body goes through some hella strange changes, a wild-ass fever, and suddenly, you're able to do insane things." She counts them on her fingers. "Shift. Breathe fire. Super strength. Elf-killing venom. Make dragon babies. And most of all… dragons live a long ass time. We're talking probably a couple hundred more years *after* mating."

"Well, that's a hell of a perk." I draw back. "Wait, you're going to outlive me."

"Unless you mate. Which I highly recommend." Her expression softens. "And if it's not Aleks, Cin… you should move on. Find the one you're meant to be with."

"That part is really fucked."

"It's not. I promise." But there's sympathy on her face. "I was lucky. Niko was the first dragon I kissed, and he was my mate. And then we were in a hurry to rescue you, which meant we needed mated dragons, and then everything moved so fast, and… I didn't have that much time to think about it. Which, in retrospect, was probably a good thing."

"Wait, back up." I frown at her. "Why did you need mated dragons to rescue me?"

She gives a small smile. "Teleportation. It's the only way to get to the Vardigah realm."

The sick feeling in my stomach is still there. "Shut up. Then why does Aleks say we don't have a good way to go back for Julia?"

"There are so few mated dragons." Ember purses her lips. "And we're so important to the survival of Niko's people—my people now. It's hard to risk that when we don't know what we're after. We didn't even know who Julia was until just now, when you got your memories back. She might not have been real. And the witch—Alice—is an unknown threat. Niko and Constantine have been fighting about it ever since we got back."

"*You* took the risk," I say just now putting it all together. "You mated just so you could take the risk to rescue someone."

"To rescue *you*," she says gently. "And I'd do it again in a heartbeat because you're my sister, so fucking shut up about that, okay?"

It kind of chokes me up, so I just nod.

"*Anyway,*" she continues, "you need to be careful with Aleks. If he's your soul mate, and you make love, you could end up mated before you realize it. And if he's not… well… you will probably break his heart, anyway. Do it quickly and move on."

"Well, that's fucked up," I protest.

"Yeah. Pretty much."

But now I *really* understand why my beautiful sister is mated to a dragon. It wasn't just that she fell in love. It wasn't simply destiny or the strong desire to help save the dragon people. *She was coming to rescue me.* And I know her—that's one thing she would risk anything for. It makes my heart swell, but it also freaks me out. The only saving grace is that she seems ridiculously happy about being mated to Niko, wildly in love, and also eager to make little dragon babies. Which is cute but also completely nuts for her.

I reach over and pull her into a sudden hug. "I love you, sis."

It must not be too awkward because her hug is fierce. "Always."

When I pull back, she's got a shine in her eyes. I give her a teasing poke. "Are you sure you're not preggers already? Ember Dubois is *not* a crier."

"Only if I'm lucky." And she means it.

I just shake my head. So much change in such a short time.

Ember pulls in a breath. "Are we good here? Because I'm really worried about Niko down there with whatever fresh hell the night has brought."

I nod and climb up from the couch, saying, "Let's go check it out." I'm glad I got things straight with my sister about this mating business, but as we work our way down to the main floor, it's clear things are horrible. A few women are softly crying. The men are standing in groups with hunched shoulders and haunted looks. A larger group is gathered in the front room, so we gravitate that way and find Niko, Constantine, Aleks and several other dragon men I don't know all standing around a man's body on the floor. One of them is kneeling, his hand on the fallen man's chest as he quietly sobs.

The man who died is beautiful, like they all are —he looks slightly surprised, like death snuck up and played a terrible joke by stealing him away from the party.

Ember gravitates to Niko, who's quietly discussing something with Constantine.

Aleks sees me and comes to my side.

"I'm so sorry." I'm not sure what else to say. I'm

sure he was one of the "brother dragons" as they seem to call each other.

"This is bad." He's shaking his head.

"Do they know what he died from?" I hope that's not too callous to ask.

The frown on his face grows darker. "Dragons don't die like this, Cinder. Certainly not *unmated* dragons. We might wither away if we never find a mate, but we don't just drop dead. If he were mated, then maybe…"

My eyes go wide. "What do you mean, if he were mated?"

He sighs and slips a hand around my waist. "There's a lot you need to know, my love. A lot I want to tell you, just as soon as we have a chance." He brushes a soft kiss across my cheek, then says quietly, "Mated dragons are mated for life. If one dies, the other perishes. Instantly. To an outsider, they appear to simply fall dead for no apparent reason. But we know what it is."

"That's… kind of awful." And it adds another whole level of weirdness to this mating business.

"It's how it works," he says like it's not awful at all. "They share one soul. When one dies, the soul is released from the body. From *both* bodies. That's the nature of being joined. But Yiannis wasn't mated. If his other half, wherever she is, died while they were unmated, her soul would be reborn in someone new. She would keep searching for him. And him for her. If he dies before he finds her, his soul departs and her dragon spirit will leave her body as well. But she would go on living because she was never fully dragon. Only her Dragon Spirit would be gone. The hope is that they will join in the great beyond. But this…" He gestures to Yiannis's body. "This doesn't make any sense. He wasn't mated. Dragons don't die of natural causes, not like this. They wither or, if they're mated, they'll both reach a peaceful end together. We call it the passing. It's usually at night when they're quiet and alone. With Yannis… it's like his spirit was somehow ripped from his body…"

My eyes go wide. "Like his soul was destroyed?"

"What? No, that can't…" He trails off at the look on my face. "What are you saying?"

A chill is settling into the pit of my stomach. "Alice said the dark elves were trying to destroy our souls—mine and Julia's. I thought she meant that *figuratively*—like the torture was supposed to break us somehow. And she was trying to heal us, support us, help us find a way out…"

"But if she meant that literally…" He looks so horrified, it chills me even more.

"Why wouldn't they just kill us?" A shiver works all the way through me. I asked myself that question a hundred times while I was captured. I just couldn't figure out *the point* of it all.

"Because your spirit would go on living," Aleks explains quickly. "You're Dragon Spirited. They had to know this. Alice must have told them. That's why they took you in the first place. All the torture… all the experimentation… if they were trying to magic a way to destroy your soul but not your body…" He looks at Yiannis's fallen form. "I think they've figured it out."

I want to huddle closer to Aleks. I want him to wrap those strong arms around me and say "my love" and tell me everything's going to be fine.

Instead, he strides with panicked steps to Niko to tell him the elves have a new weapon against the dragons: *killing the souls of their mates.*

I wrap my arms around myself to contain my full-body shudder.

SEVEN

Aleksandr

"Don't leave without me," I say to Niko.

He's deep into planning the assault on the
Vardigah with the other mated dragons—Ember,
Renn, and Ketu—and a half dozen unmated ones,
including Constantine. "Are you going to see her?"
Niko asks me from across the room. He means
Cinder.

Because *yes*, I'm going to see her. Obviously. I'm
just not sure what I'm going to say.

"Yeah." I turn to stride out of his office.

"Wait up!" he calls and comes jogging after me.

I keep walking until I'm out in the game room. I
know what he wants to say, and I'd rather not do it
in front of everyone. I sent Cinder back to the
cottage last night—she needed to rest, and there

wouldn't be much of that. Not with everyone on edge, just waiting for the next dragon to drop. She didn't want to go, but I insisted. And I sent Ember with her, although she soon returned. The consensus seems to be that all the mated dragons are safe—it's the unmated ones, like me, Constantine, and virtually every other dragon in the house, who feel the sharp blade of destiny hanging over our necks.

Niko meets me around the corner from the office serving as our impromptu war room. "What're you going to do?" he asks. As if he doesn't know.

"Tell her I love her."

"She already knows that." He fucking growls at me.

Well, don't ask stupid questions, then. I keep that inside. I'm on edge, like everyone else. Although no more dragons have dropped dead, which means two things: that Yiannis's soul mate was likely Julia and that Julia's Dragon Spirit is now gone. Which also means Julia's probably dead, knowing the Vardigah and their sentimentality about keeping people alive who are useless to them.

"Then I'll just have to seduce her into loving me, too." Last night, I told him that Cinder was my soul mate—*after* the initial panic about Yiannis had settled. He didn't believe me. No, that's not right—he asked if she felt the connection, too. When I said I didn't know, that I hadn't told her yet, that's when he said her Dragon Spirit might already be dead.

I wanted to punch him. I almost did—I walked out of the strategy meeting and took a very long hike around the island. Then I came back and pretended to sleep for the rest of the night. Finally, after punching the hell out of some training equipment in the gym, I came back to the office, but only to tell him I was leaving.

If Cinder's Dragon Spirit is already dead—if the Vardigah succeeded with all their torture—then I'm not her soul mate and never was. It was just my ardent wishful thinking all along. Some other dragon in the world dropped dead some time ago. Maybe a rogue. Maybe someone in another lair. We'll never know.

But I refuse to believe what I see in my best friend's eyes—that I'm making up this feeling, this *connection*, I have with her. That I'm simply a fool of a dragon, in love and hopelessly wishing I've finally found my soul mate.

"Aleks, I'm sorry about what I said," Niko starts.

I wave him off. I don't want to hear it. "I'm going." I turn again to leave.

Niko catches my arm. *"My brother…"*

I yank out of his hold. But then I stop and stare at the carpet. "I have to try, Niko. I have to *know.*"

"I understand." His voice is soft. "You don't need to come on this mission. Besides, Constantine wants to go *now.*"

"You need dragons who've been there before." I glare at him. "A few more hours won't matter. Don't leave without me."

He gives me a pinched look, probably calculating why I want to go so badly on a mission that's possibly one-way and dangerous no matter what. And I could give all kinds of plausible reasons. We have to make sure the witch, Alice, doesn't guide the Vardigah to kidnapping any more soul mates. If we don't eliminate that threat, any of us could drop dead at any moment. We should at least try to find Julia, if she's not already dead—maybe Alice knows. If Julia's alive and still Dragon Spirited, we need to get her out of the Vardigah's clutches before they kill her soul, too. And finally, because I've had Niko's back on every single thing for two hundred years, and notwithstanding that I hate him for what he said—for what he *believes* about how foolish I am—I will not let him go into battle without me by his side.

All of that is true.

But that's not why I need to go—it's because if Cinder isn't my soul mate, then I'm done. Done looking. Done waiting. Either she'll have me or she won't. I don't want to rush her, but I already know —this is it for me. If it doesn't work with her, I'm going out in a blaze of glory and Vardigah blood on the wall. I already have plenty of reasons to hate them, but knowing what they did to Cinder—*especially* if they killed her Dragon Spirit—means they've destroyed any hope I have in this realm. And I will make them pay for it.

I say none of this, but Niko has to know. We've been brother-cousins for two hundred years.

"Okay," he says finally. "We'll wait for you."

I give him a sharp nod and turn away.

It's daylight now, so I can't simply fling myself off the balcony and fly to Cinder with the intent of making love to her for hours on end. That chance passed when her memories awoke. Which feels like a metaphor for our entire relationship—a chance that didn't quite work out. The first time I told her about my world sent her reeling back into that unconscious state. The first time I almost kissed her,

I ran away, desperate to extend the romance we had started. And then when I finally climbed into her bed, the past reared up and destroyed any hope of being together.

But Cinder's worth fighting for—more than worth it. And I'm running out of time.

The ride over on the motorboat feels dark, even though the sun is shining on the water. When I reach the island and tie up, I hesitate before heading up to the cottage. Ember's back at the lair, but there will be staff on hand. I head for the front door instead of coming in the back, as was my original intent. I find Biti and ask her to take the day and tell the rest of the staff, too. That I want some alone time with Cinder. She refrains from saying anything, just gives me a knowing smile, and scurries off to clear out the place.

On her way out, Biti tells me Cinder's in the garden.

I knock on the bedroom door, just in case, but it's empty. The sliding glass door is still open, letting in the fresh, warm breeze and the scent of the flowers. I step through the open space, shading my eyes. She's down on the wooden bench swing under the pergola, lazily pushing at the pavers with her bare toes. I just watch her for a moment, the sway of her white cotton skirt rocking with the motion of the swing. This is it—the perfect moment.

I trot down the steps to the path, so she'll hear me coming.

She's up out of the swing by the time I get there. "Hey! I didn't expect—"

I don't bother with words, I just pull her body against mine and kiss her, long and deep. Her hands slide to my back, holding me in. We're melded together for a long moment, reconnecting, her mouth on mine, my hands in her hair and at the small of her back. I'm hard for her, *always*, and that rapidly becomes clear with how close we're pressed together. I want her—my mouth is aching for her— but a few things have to be said first.

I fist my hand in her hair to pull back from the kiss—she's as hungry for this as I am. "Cinder, I'm so fucking gone for you." Not the most romantic thing to say, but—

"Oh, Aleks." Her fingers dig into my back. "I've been so worried."

Fuck. I'm messing this up. I relax my grip on her hair and nuzzle her cheek. "I didn't mean to make you worry," I whisper then gaze into those beautiful eyes. "Everything inside me says you're meant to be mine. That if I was ever to have a soul mate in this world, you're it. But I can't be sure. I can't *know.* Not until…" How can I say this? Take the risk of being bonded to me for life? Just so I can find out if it's possible?

But she's nodding. "Not until we make love. Ember explained it to me."

Relief gushes through me. At least she understands. "You might not even be…" I swallow. "The Vardigah might have destroyed your Dragon Spirit. What I'm feeling—this *connection*—it might just be left over from what was there before."

"But if it's not…" She's looking deep into my eyes. "And we make love, we might mate. We might bond. I might become a dragon. Aleks… I understand. I'm willing to take that risk."

It stabs me at the same time my heart soars. Because I don't want it to be something she's *risking*… I want it to be something she *wants.* "My love… it won't work if you're not in love with me, and I don't want to rush you, and I know it's only been a few days, but we're going on this raid and—"

"Aleks." She grabs hold of my cheeks to stop me from talking. "I love everything you are. Make love to me. Right now. *Please."*

And there is zero chance of me saying no to that.

I bring her mouth back to mine, devouring her with my kiss. I groan as my other hand finds her breast, heavy and soft. I shove aside the silky fabric of her blouse, hungry for the feel of her skin. I dip my head to taste the hard bud of her nipple, now free in the fresh air, as she clasps my head to her breast.

"Oh, *fuck*, Aleks. I've been dreaming about this." Her head is tipped back with the pleasure of me merely lapping at her breast.

"Yeah?" I say, voice husky. I grab her cute little behind to steady her against my shoulder and kneel down to slip my hand under her long, sweeping skirt. That needs to come off or at least *up*. "What have you been dreaming of? *Specifically.*" I've got her skirt up to her waist, revealing soft white-lace panties. Her hands dig in my hair as I kiss the soft flesh of her thighs, slipping my tongue under the edge of the silk cloth.

"On the bench." Her voice is raspy. "I want your cock inside me as I swing."

Goddammit. I was going to take this slow, but not when she's talking like that. I stand up, slipping my hand into her panties as I go. "Let's see what we can do about that." I kiss her—my tongue invading her mouth, my fingers pressing into the wet softness between her legs—and walk her the few steps back to the bench. She's panting, and her soft whimper goes straight to my cock. I release her so I can slide down her panties. My hands skim the softness of her legs on the way back up, lifting her skirt again.

I reach her hips and grab hold. "Sit down and spread your legs for me."

I can feel her shudder in my hands, but she does as she's told. I kneel down and spread her even wider, hooking my forearms under her knees and grabbing the edge of the bench. Then I bury my face between her legs, lapping at her hot sex, using the bench to swing her just a small way into the eagerness of my tongue. She shrieks, then moans, then starts saying my name like a fucking prayer. I devour her, licking and sucking with no mercy because I need this woman to come on my face *now*. And that's just a start. I have so many more things to do with her.

She's writhing and cursing. I know she's close. Her sweet nub is swollen, her sex is blossoming like a flower with all the attention, and I could stay here for days. But she *specifically* requested my cock, and I'm dying to give her just that. I clamp down and suck hard. Her scream is satisfyingly loud as she bucks into my face, convulsing and coming with tremors and twitches that make me grin. I hope the staff made it off the island—otherwise, they definitely know what we're doing. I pull back, all smiles, and check out the sated beauty on the swing. Arms limp at her sides, legs wide and her sex beautifully displayed. Her lips are parted, eyelids heavy, a slight flush in her cheeks that *I* caused. I take no small amount of pride in making any woman come, but *this woman...* this woman's orgasmic glow on a garden bench is like an erotic Renaissance painting.

"Oh, fuck. *Aleks.*" She says it with her eyes still mostly closed.

"Was that your fantasy, my love?" I stand, toe off my shoes, and rip my shirt over my head.

"No, but *fuck...* it should have been."

I start unbuttoning my jeans, releasing my poor, aching cock from its prison. She opens her eyes and peers up at me with the most deliciously mischievous smirk. She reaches for my cock.

"Hang on, that's not—" The rest is strangled by her tongue lapping a long lick from the base of my shaft to the tip. *"Fuck."* She takes me in her hand and into her mouth. The garden disappears. The pergola with its hanging vines, the flowering bushes and ferns, even the erotic promise of the bench swing—all of it is gone. All I can see is Cinder's lips wrapped around my cock while it slides in and out. She's devouring me, taking me deeper with each pass. My hands find her hair, gently holding her head, letting her set the pace—I'm just along for this ball-tightening ride. She laps then sucks then flicks her tongue across my tip. She's performing a whole tongue dance on my cock, and it's making me so fucking hard. Which is perfect for what comes next—and which is not going to be *me*. Unless I let this go on too long, then I'm definitely coming deep in her throat. Which I 100% need to do in the near future, but not right now. Not yet.

"Cinder," I warn. *Fuck,* she's getting me there fast.

"Mmm?" she hums. Then she just takes me deeper.

Oh, God. I tighten my grip on her head and slowly pull her away. "Enough of that. I need to be inside you. And not *this* way."

She gives a whimper of complaint, but she releases me. I grab her hands and lift her from where she'd sunk to her knees. I dip down to lift her skirt again and ease her back toward the swing. "I want you right here," I say as I set her perched on the edge. "Lean back." I kneel between her legs. The bench is at just the right height. She braces her hand against the back, but I tip her further still by hooking my arms under her knees and bringing her sweet sex to the very edge of the bench, right up against the tip of my cock. "A little help, my love," I pant as I grip the bench, ready to impale her with my cock by swinging her onto it. She reaches her long fingers between us and lines us up, guiding just the tip into her hot wetness.

"Oh, God," she breathes, but I'm barely inside her.

She's squirming for more, and I have a fantasy I need to deliver. So I grip the bench and pull it hard, impaling her with one swift stroke. *So fucking tight.* She shrieks again, her free hand grabbing at my chest, fingers digging in.

"Holy *fuck*, Aleks!" she hisses.

I swing the bench away and then back again, hard. And again.

She whimpers.

"You are *mine,*" I say through gritted teeth because *fuck* she's so tight. The look of surprise and wordless pleasure on her face are making me lose my mind. Making me want to work this bench even harder. *"Mine,"* I say as I pick up the pace, jerking the bench toward me, piercing her again and again with my cock. "I don't care… what the universe says…" I pant, holding rock-solid still as I crash her and the bench against me. "You're meant to be *mine*. Riding my cock. Every day." Her whimper is punctuated by the jostling of me, the bench, my cock—all of it one giant, rhythmic fuck. Her hand moves to my shoulder, gripping me, the other holding fast to the back of the bench, each trying to keep from sliding out of this perfect rhythm we have going. I'm getting close. I need her to come, *and come now*, because I'm far from finished with this.

"I love you, baby," I pant, still pounding. "You've got my cock. My heart. Fucking all of me. Now *come* for me!" I angle to take her just a little deeper, and she suddenly gasps and sits practically upright on the swing.

"Oh fuck oh fuck!!" Then she wraps her arms around my neck, pulling herself up off the swing, and I hold her deep as she convulses around my cock. The bench swings free behind her as she clutches me and comes and comes. Once again, I'm swept into the beauty of her, the raw femininity, as her body clings to me, clenches my cock, and she rides it through to the very last wave.

"Oh, God," she breathes when the frenzy has passed.

"You're so fucking beautiful," I whisper as I rub my rough cheek against her soft one. "But I'm not done with you."

"I… what are you…" She sputters in the cutest way as I slowly rise up from my knees, bringing her with me. Then I unhook her legs from around my back and lower her to the ground. Her bare feet are so adorable. Note to self: lick those little toes. Later.

"Turn around." I gently nudge her until she's facing the swing. I sweep her gorgeous hair to the front and kiss the back of her neck while kneading her breasts from behind. There are too many things I want to do. Too many ways I want to have her. I have a sense that there's not enough *time*… but I shove that away. I know just the fantasy *I* have of her and the bench, and I want it now. "On the bench. On your knees," I whisper along the sweet skin at the back of her neck.

She stumbles forward. I grin at the looseness of her limbs, knowing I caused it. And I'm going to keep doing that as long as I can. She kneels on the bench, hands gripping the back, half bent over. The skirt is protecting her knees, but they're not spread far enough. I reach down to gather up all the folds of her skirt and push them up until her beautiful behind is exposed, and she's bared to me. She looks back at me, eyelids still at half-mast, the pleasure still slacking her expression.

"Are you going to—"

"Hell yes." I pet her, running my hand the length of her wetness, spreading her wider, and her fingers dig into the bench. Then I take hold of her hips, position the tip of my cock at her entrance, and slowly pull her onto me. I'm not holding the swing, so she has to steel herself—digging her knees into the dip of the seat, gripping the back of the bench, so she doesn't slip off. All I'm doing is pulling her sweet body into mine, the swing responding with the smallest arc. I time it so my cock smoothly slips into her, right with the pace of the swing. Simple. Natural. Like it was always meant to be.

"Oh… *Aleks…*"

"Yes, my love?" I'm just calmly fucking her like this is just what we do on a Sunday morning in the pergola. In and out. The slow steadiness of it is tightening everything inside me.

"Have I told you…" She shudders, and it's so delicious. I feel it along the length of my cock and in my hands gripping her hips. "Have I said… how much I like your cock?"

"How much?" I pull a little harder, stepping up the frequency of the swing.

"So. Much. *Uhnn.*" That last part is for the bump up in speed. "God, you're big."

"It's all for you, baby." And I know that's literally true now. I can't have *this* and ever be with someone else. There's no other woman in the universe for me. "I'm sorry," I pant as I ratchet up the rhythm of the swing. "But I need to just fuck you right now."

"*Oh, God, yes.*" She bends a little, thrusting her behind out just a touch, gripping even harder on the bench as I plunge into her. I grit my teeth, trying to hold it off, but the sight of her sweet bottom, my cock slamming into her, harder and harder, the incredibly tight hotness that is *her*… and I'm about to shoot off.

This is every fantasy I've ever had and ever will. "Baby," I gasp, "I'm coming. *Fuck.*" I tip over the edge, slamming into her with my cock and then my whole body as I pitch her forward, grab the bench and then hold her hard as I empty into her.

She whimpers and shudders, and suddenly, I can

feel her convulsing around my cock. I hold her and the bench, both of us gripping the back to stay upright, me buried deep inside her as I spill and spill. Even when I'm empty, my cock seems to keep trying, still twitching as she works through her orgasm. When I haven't anything left, and her waves stop coming, I finally release my rock-hard grip on her.

"You okay?" I ask, as I pull out and bring her up to standing with me, suddenly concerned I might have bruised her with all my fervent owning of her body.

She just nods, but I can tell she's overwhelmed. I bend down to lift her, curling her to my chest and carrying her bridal style away from the bench and the pergola. Her hair spills against my skin. Her face nuzzles into my shoulder. She's the most precious treasure I've ever held in my arms, and I want more than anything to keep her forever.

But as I climb the steps to her balcony and her room, I know one thing *didn't* happen in the garden just now: *Cinder Dubois didn't turn dragon.*

Which means she's not my soul mate after all.

EIGHT

Cinder

I'm floating in a post-orgasm haze.

Aleks's finger traces a gentle line down my arm, along the curve of my breast, up to my collarbone and back down my arm. "You're so beautiful," he murmurs. He's been saying things like that since he carried me into the cottage and to the bed. We're cuddled together, warm and pleasantly exhausted from the most amazing love-making I've ever experienced. Aleks is straight-up hot, so that's been firing my engines from the first time I saw him. But *three* orgasms in one round? And not just ordinary ones, either, but leg-shaking, body-convulsing ecstasies that I'm still recovering from. And speaking of recovery—his cock was everything it promised from the pictures. I'm pleasantly sore and yet still up for more. I'd start an Aleks's Cock Admiration Club, pledging a sincere commitment to worshipping that lovely appendage, but I don't want to share with anyone. I'd like more of that taste I got earlier, but that will have to wait.

Right now is sweet-loving time.

He's propped up on pillows at the head of the bed, that gorgeous cock lying thick and soft off to the side of his ridiculously muscular body. I've dated men who were solid, even a couple who were weight lifters, but Aleks is in a class by himself. Every ripple of muscle is pronounced. His skin is supple and soft, but there's only steel underneath. I'm snuggled up to his side, resting my head on his chest, which is slowly rising and falling with his breathing. His words rumble deep inside. He's playing with my hair now, strewing it across his body. I think he likes the feel of it. I like the feel of *him*, so I trace my own lines of touch, just with my fingertips, down his belly and toward that cock I'd like to worship. It's funny because I've always been a fan of cocks, but not like this. Once again, Aleks is in a class by himself.

I lightly circle the tip with my finger.

He bunches his fist in my hair in response. *"Cinder, my love."* There's warning in his voice that sends a pulse of pleasure between my legs. He doesn't even have to touch me to manage that.

I nibble on his chest then grin up at him. He's looking down, eyes fixed on my fingers, which are now playing along his length like a flute. He turns those beautiful gray eyes to me—they're darkened, and his eyelids are heavy with lust.

"You're playing with fire."

"Is that what you shoot out of that thing? Because it was *hot.*" He growls in that low and sexy way and snatches my hand away from his cock. Then he rolls me over on my back and nibbles on my breasts while holding my wrist above my head. "Oh, is that how it's going to be?" I ask, then squirm against him because I'm already aching to have him between my legs again.

He draws in a deep breath, nuzzling against my breast as he does so, then he releases me and props himself up, putting a tiny bit of distance between our bodies. "We need to talk."

"Well, *that* sounds like zero fun." He's been somber ever since we came inside. I don't know why, but something isn't right. It took me a few minutes to notice it because I was lost in the glow. I smirk at him. "I'd rather see what my tongue can do to make you hot and bothered."

He smiles. "You make me hot and bothered when you use it to talk."

"You are such a liar."

"In fact, I am not." He's still grinning as he runs his thumb across my lower lip. "But you have no idea how hard it is to turn down that offer, even temporarily."

"How temporarily?" I twist to face him and place my hand on the delicious muscular curve of his chest. Slowly, purposefully, I head south.

He lifts my hand and laces his fingers with mine. "How are you so perfect for me?" But he says it wistfully, which makes me frown.

"I'm sure I'm not the first to admire you and your package."

He chuckles and squeezes my fingers and leans in to kiss me. It's soft. Gentle. So sweet and loving, I have a sudden ache in my chest when he pulls away. *Why is he sad?* We just made the most perfect love, we fit perfectly together... why does it feel like he's winding up to *Goodbye?*

He sighs. "You're not a dragon, my love."

"Um... *yeah.* I know? *You're* the dragon. I feel like this is a trick question."

He frowns and gives me a look like I should get this. I scan his eyes for some clue then try to focus on something other than his otherworldly hotness. The only way I could be a dragon is if—

"Oh." A chill washes through me. "Was I supposed to… was it supposed to happen that fast?"

He nods, and it's so sad, it makes tears prick at the back of my eyes. "If you were my soul mate," he says, "we'd be mated by now. You'd be transformed—and that's not something you'd miss, no matter how blissed out you were. That only leaves two possibilities."

"What?" Now I'm propped up too, the chill taking residence in the pit of my stomach.

"Either you're someone else's soul mate—which makes me crazy if I think about it for even half a second—or the Vardigah managed to kill your Dragon Spirit."

"Oh, shit, do you think…"

"I wasn't sure you'd even wake up, my love." He strokes my cheek. "It's very possible they managed to kill your dragon soul."

"But I thought you said—"

"I wanted it to be true." He shakes his head and looks away. "I was desperate to believe you were my soul mate. That the connection I felt was a soul bond. But the truth is I'd fallen for you long before that kiss."

"So, what does that mean?" My heart is starting to race. Because he's acting like this means we can't be together and that's crazy to me. This whole soul mate business was suspicious from the start. But if it means two people who love each other—who are perfect for each other—can't be together, well then that's just *wrong*.

His gaze comes back, and he lifts a long strand of my hair, letting it run through his fingers. "It means my soul mate is still out there somewhere. Otherwise, I'd be dead like Yiannis. But it's not like I have much time left to find her. And now that I've found you…" His beautiful eyes find mine. "I don't want anyone else, Cinder. You're it for me."

My heart swells, and I press a hand to his cheek, then a kiss to his lips. It's a kiss that makes me want to cry. Because it's not fate. It's not soul mates. It's *me* that he wants. And somehow that makes all the difference. I think I was holding back before. I told him I loved everything he was—and that was true —but I'm not sure I truly loved *him* until this moment.

When I pull back from my desperate kissing, he says, "But I don't think you want me, my love."

"*What?* Are you insane? You're all I want."

But he shakes his head like I'm still not getting

it. "Dragons my age are starting to wither—there aren't many left of my generation, the first and oldest. Constantine is one. And he's got the right idea—take the battle to the Vardigah, stop the witch from wayfinding soul mates for them, and keep anyone else like Yiannis, younger dragons who still have hope, from dropping dead because the dark elves have killed the souls of their mates. This I can do. And while I'm there, I'm going to avenge what they did to you. I don't know if they destroyed your dragon spirit or just tortured your beautiful mind, but either way, I'd really like to make them pay."

"*No.*" I slam my hand against his chest and then grip on, like I'm not going to physically let him go. "You do *not* have to go on some vengeance quest for me. You *stay here* and you *love me.*" The tears are pushing their way out, and I have to bite my lip to keep it from trembling.

"*Shhh,*" he says, pushing back my hair and kissing my forehead. "Are you sure you want me?"

"Yes!"

"Even if it's just a short while?"

"*Aleks.*"

"Even if you have to watch me wither away to nothing?" He's holding me close, but I can hear him choking up. "Wouldn't it be better if I simply didn't come back?"

"No, that would *not* be better." I slam my hand against his chest again. "And *fuck you* for thinking that." This time I struggle against him, his massive weight making anything impossible, but he gets the idea and lets me push him onto his back. I straddle him and plant my hands on him and stare him down from above. "Did you or did you not stay by my bedside for *two fucking weeks* when I was a feverish wreck of a woman?"

"That was different—"

"*Hell yes,* it was different!" I'm shouting at him. He wisely buttons it. "You didn't even know me. I was just some chick who was out of her mind. But you stayed by me. You talked to me. You brought me fucking *flowers…*" I glance at the fresh ones that are still there from the last time he plucked them from the garden and brought them in. I'm seriously starting to cry. I turn back to him, eyes brimming. "You listened to me. You held me. You *cried* for me, Aleks, and I swear to you, there's no way I would be healed and whole and fucking *in love* right now if it weren't for you. So don't sit there and tell me what I want or what I'm willing to do for you. *I want it all.*

And I want it right now. And I'll take it for every second that it lasts."

His eyes are glassing up, and we're both a mess, so I grab hold of him and lean forward and kiss him with everything I've got. His hands are on me, but they're too gentle. Too soft. I want to love him *hard.* Just so he gets the right idea, I push up from the kiss and settle back down on his body, grinding right where it feels best—on that gorgeous cock of his. And it's already coming to life. I feel it growing hard under me. Aleks is groaning now, his hands cupping my breasts and pinching my nipples.

"Fuck, *Cinder,* you feel so good." He's looking down where our bodies meet, and I want him to know exactly what he's getting with me. President and only member of the Appreciation of Aleks's Cock Club. So I slide down his body, and that gorgeous cock springs up. He groans even before I take him in my mouth, but I aim to make him do that even more. He's thick and super hard—it takes two hands and my mouth to do a proper job, but that's what I'm doing. *"Fuck!"* he cries out. "Holy— *ahhh!"* He's squirming under me, so I lean my elbow into his stomach to make him lie still. He just curls up, and now I'm giving him head in his lap while he holds my hair and watches. I give him all the show I can. He's panting and swearing and saying things like *Fuck me Fuck me,* so I think I'm doing all right. His cock is twitching in my hands—he's got to be close.

"Cinder, *stop!*"

I jerk up to look at him, alarmed. *"What?"*

"You're going to make me come!"

"That's the idea, you big dork!"

He just growls and lifts me up, turning me and somehow pinning me face down on the bed, my wrists above my head. He straddles me, and I have no idea where he's going with this until I feel his cock slide past my rear end and into my already-wet sex from behind. I gasp as he fills me, this angle so different and deep. He slowly glides all the way in, his hands still holding my wrists, keeping him up while he's fully seated inside me.

"You like that?" He's breathless.

I just push up into him, which makes me whimper because that only brings him deeper.

"Hold still, my love, while I fuck you until you can't stand."

Oh, fuck, yes. He pulls out slow but then slams back in. "Fuck!" I yelp. He pulls out and thrusts again. "Yes, yes, yes." I'm saying it through gritted teeth as he fucking *pounds* into me. He's grunting with every thrust now, groaning in between, and generally taking me so hard and fast, he's shaking the bed with us, pounding it against the wall. I'm gasping for air, crying out as the pressure builds, because this isn't an orgasm, it's a tsunami of pleasure building from my toes to my sex to my wrists pinned to the bed. When it finally peaks and lets loose, I scream and buck back into him, arching and pushing, hardly even in control of my body. He releases my wrists and wraps his arm around my chest as I arch up. In this position, it's like we're melded together as one, his front to my back, one quivering, orgasmic body. He's still pounding, still working my body, still burying himself in me, and just as my own orgasm slows, he drops us both down to the bed, buried deep, holding still and *shaking* as he empties into me. He's shivering against my backside, his groans so deep and erotic, I nearly come again just listening to it. But mostly I'm floating away on an incredible high... and hot as hell. Like literally drenching hot. This position has heated me up *insanely*, even after the orgasm has ebbed away.

"Oh, baby. Oh, my love," Aleks is whispering in my ear, moving my hair so he can reach my face to kiss me. Then he pulls back. "You okay?"

I'm still breathing hard. "I'm just hot. You're a fucking *god* in bed, Aleks. Did I mention this?"

"You're *what?*" He pulls out—which is no small thing because Aleks's cock is one of the eighth wonders of the world. My body cries a little when he leaves. But he's turning me over, and the fresh breeze on my *on fire* body is a slice of heaven too, so I let him.

Shit, the bed is soaked with my sweat. How embarrassing. Then again, Aleks did this to me, so…

"Cinder." His voice is so alarmed, I open my eyes. He's sitting up.

"What?"

There's blank surprise on his face. "I thought it was just… I thought it was just the sex…"

"What in the world are you saying?" I prop myself up on my elbows. The extra air across my skin feels *glorious.* I think I'm finally cooling down.

"We're mated." A grin slowly spreads across his face.

"I'm sorry, what?" The sex has fuzzed out his brain.

He scrambles off the bed.

I frown. "Where are you going—"

He disappears.

"Aleks!" My heart lurches, and I bolt straight up.

He reappears again with a goofy grin on his face. He's holding a white flower. From the garden.

"What the—"

"Teleportation." He's positively giddy, climbing on the bed again.

"Are you fucking kidding me?" I take the daisy from him, but my mouth is hanging open.

He grabs my face in both hands and kisses me. I can feel his smile through it.

Then he pulls back. "I… I don't understand it." But he's insanely happy. "You try."

"Try *what?*" I'm just gaping at him. There's no fucking way I can teleport.

"Try *shifting.*" He's pulling me by the hands out of bed. "You can do it now. We're *mated,* Cinder!" He grabs me and kisses me again.

I don't understand how this is suddenly possible. After he told me it wasn't. But he really, really wants me to do this. Under the excitement, there's disbelief—wariness? Like I need to prove to him this is real or he won't believe. Hell, I don't believe it.

I set the daisy on the bed. "How do I shift?" I'd do anything for this man.

He steps back, hands pressed together and held to his lips. "Think about Ember. Remember when she shifted? She's your twin. Close your eyes and picture it's you shifting instead."

I frown but close my eyes and try to remember that day. My sister freaked me the hell out by turning into a golden dragon right in front of me. That was the start of this whole wild adventure. Makes sense to end it this way too. I picture it and try and focus... but nothing. I hear Aleks laughing, so I open my eyes, ready to tell him it's not that easy, but—

I'm fucking up in the air.

Wait, no...

Holy shit, I'm a dragon! My neck is so long that my head is bumping the ceiling but down below I can see two long legs with golden metallic scales and super sharp talons. *Shit, shit, shit.* I close my eyes and wish myself human again with the fervent, freaked-out hope of Dorothy trying to get home.

When I peek again, I'm back at normal height, a plain, naked human.

"Yes! That is what I'm talking about!" Aleks sweeps me up in his arms and spins me around. Then he tumbles us onto the bed and curls me up tight in his arms. "I can't believe it," he says, all smiles. "Maybe it just took one more time of making love? I mean, that makes *no* sense, but nothing else changed. You had to have always been my soul mate. You already loved me. Maybe it's just the orgasm—was it stronger this time for you, too? I swear, there was some freaky magic this time like it was just resonating…" He trails off at the look on my face. "What's wrong?"

"I'm kind of freaked out by being a dragon." Which is true, but that's not why there's a vaguely horrified look on my face.

"Oh, baby, I'm sorry." He cuddles me up, pulling me with him to the head of the bed. And it does help to be in his arms. There's something about his touch—there always has been, even from that first memory, back when I first woke up. His touch is *soothing.* "I'm just… I can't believe it," he says. "You've literally saved me." He cups my cheek again and kisses me so sweetly that I know I have to tell him. I do. But I don't want to.

I wait until he pulls back and kisses me lightly on the nose. "No more shifting," he says. "Not until you're ready. I shouldn't have rushed you. I'm always fucking doing that—"

"Aleks."

He stops at the tone of my voice. "What?"

"I know why it didn't work the first time." My

heart has a stabbing pain, which is silly, maybe, but it still hurts to say this. "I lied."

He frowns like I'm not making sense. "Lied about what?"

I swallow then touch his face, just with the tips of my fingers. "I don't think I was truly in love with you until *after*... until I knew you truly wanted me. Just me. Not my dragon spirit. Not being mated. Just... *me.*"

He's still confused. "That's it?"

"What do you mean *that's it?* I said I loved you and I... well, kind of didn't totally."

He smiles. Then he laughs. Then he cracks up so hard he's falling over on the bed.

"Okay, there's something really wrong with you," I say. And I'm kind of miffed.

"I'm sorry." But he's still laughing. Trying not to, but still. "I'm sorry, baby." He calms a little and cuddles me up again. And I *do* love him—*now*—so I let him. And don't even smack him. He kisses my forehead and says, "You're so freaking perfect for me. But of course, you are. You're my other half." He tips my head up to look at him. "You feel it, right? The connection?"

"Yeah." And I do. His love and care and attention healed me before—brought me back from all the wounds and scars from the real world and the unreal one—but making love to him just now was an entirely different thing. I feel whole in a way I never have in my life.

"So the fact that you *didn't* know if we were soul mates, and you still took the leap… that you *didn't* love me and still took the risk… do you have any idea how amazing that makes you, my beloved Dragon Spirit?"

"I… um… not really." I thought he would be mad.

He laughs again and pushes me back flat on the bed, hovering over me and staring down into my eyes. "Then you'll have to trust me. You're amazing." He kisses me softly, then his expression grows serious. "You complete me, Cinder Dubois. Your soul is my soul. Your heart beats with mine. You are the greatest treasure I will ever have."

I just stare because I have no idea what to say to that.

He smiles. "I've been waiting my whole life to say those words."

"Does that mean I'm in some kind of dragon club now?"

He laughs, and the sound of it buoys my heart. It's so full of joy.

"Yes!" He growls and nips at my neck. "The club of incredibly hot mated dragons who have unbelievable sex and make adorable baby dragons."

"Okay, we're going to have to talk about babies."

He pulls back and grins. "Might be a little late for that."

I roll my eyes. "What? Your super potent dragon seed has already got me knocked up?"

He shrugs like it's possible. He's just that studly. "Just to be sure…" His hand snakes down between my legs. "I think we should practice some more."

"Are you kidding me?" But then he strokes me, and I can't believe how good it feels. How natural. Like, of course, I should be able to make love endlessly to this amazing man. I should be sore like crazy. I should be freaked out about being a dragon and having dragon babies and fucking *teleportation*. But when Aleks slides down my body and replaces the slow tease of his hands with the magic of his tongue, I'm not thinking about anything at all…

Except how with Aleks, I won the soul mate lottery.

NINE

Aleksandr

I'M STILL HIGH. *I'M A MATED DRAGON.* IT'S LIKE A dream.

I'm blissed out from hours of incredible sex, bonding with my soul mate, and knowing that Cinder will always be mine. Literally. Until the day both our hearts stop beating. Which might be today given we're going back to the Vardigah's realm.

"I feel way too good for putting on this suit again," I say to Niko, who's standing next to me in the meeting room as we prep for the mission. I triple-check the straps on my fireproof suit—the one that keeps out the magical fire of the dark elves. Niko's doing the same, Constantine too, and Ember's helping Cinder with her suit.

"I know exactly what you mean, my brother." Niko pulls on his gloves and checks the bindings.

"And, hey, *fuck you* for thinking this wouldn't work out between Cinder and me," I say as I inspect the helmet. "Did I tell you that already?"

He smirks. "Once or twice." He slides on his own helmet and clicks on the mic. "No one's happier than I am that you're truly soul mates, Aleks."

"Yeah, no one except *me*," I throw back. "I'm definitely happier than you about this."

He just rolls his eyes.

"Are they at it again?" Cinder asks, her voice slightly muffled because I've got my helmet on and she doesn't.

"Constantly." Ember checks her sister's fireproof suit, which is the only acceptable alternative to me doing it myself. And I might still go check. "I'd tell them to get a room and kiss and make up if I didn't know for certain they're both straight as arrows."

I just blink and stare at the two women across the room. Then I say through the mic, quietly to Niko, "Having our mates be twins isn't going to go well for us, is it?"

"Not at all," he replies on the mic, just as quiet. "Are you just now figuring this out?"

"I can hear you," Ember says. Her visor is up, but she's still hooked into the helmet system.

"What are they saying?" Cinder asks.

"That they're going to get serious about this mission, right boys?" Ember throws us a pinched look.

"I'm serious!" I protest.

"You are *never* serious," Niko says, but it's light. And not entirely wrong.

"Time for a mic check," says Constantine, who is *actually* serious. Like a fucking heart attack. All the time, not just when we're off to raid the Vardigah again. "Everyone sound off."

Cinder finally has her helmet on, so we go through a round of *heres* to make sure we're all in the loop.

"All right," Niko says. "Let's go over the plan once more."

Ember and Cinder stroll around the conference table to join Niko, Constantine, and me in the open area of the meeting room. We're all mated except Constantine, so technically, we could all travel independently except for him, only we need Cinder to guide us. Which means staying close together. Niko opted for a small team again, given how tight the quarters were last time, when we rescued Cinder.

Plus there's no reason to risk more mated dragons than necessary.

I slide a hand around her waist, just because I can't stop touching her, even through a bulky fireproof suit. "You look hot in that," I say, leaning my helmet against hers.

"Shut up."

"I'm just saying that helmet is doing something for me."

"I told you—no more blow jobs until you—"

"Horny mated dragons!" Niko calls out. "Can we focus, please?" But he's laughing at us. And I can't quite kill my grin. Even though I really should. This is fucking serious.

"The plan…" Ember says with a pointed scowl I can see through her visor, which is now down. "Is that we all teleport together, hands linked, with Cinder taking us to wherever Julia is. If she can't sense Julia's presence—for example, if the Vardigah have already killed her—then I'll take point and guide us to Alice, the witch."

"And then I'll kill her," Constantine says.

There's a shocked beat of silence, then Niko says, pointedly, *"Before Constantine kills anyone,* we'll ask nicely if Alice would like to come with us."

"And if she says no," Constantine says coolly, "I'll take off her head."

Cinder scowls at him. "She's not going to say no."

Constantine pulls a dagger out of a sheath strapped to the thigh of his suit. "Tipped with dragon venom. Got it from Ketu." He sheaths it again. "No more brother dragons will die because a witch betrayed us."

I sigh, just audibly enough to have it go through the mic. "We don't know that."

"Constantine's just prepared," Niko says tightly. "As we all should be. But frankly, we only got out unscathed the last time because Alice was there and took the brunt of the Vardigah's attack with her shield. We need to make this fast, all right? I want us all home, making dragon babies *asap.*" But then he winces because obviously Constantine isn't in the mated dragon club capable of making babies.

But I am. I give a wide grin to Cinder. She just rolls her eyes. But I know she's into it, despite her protest that babies can wait. She was adamant about coming on the mission, in spite of the risks of that. Which I completely understand. She still lives with regret about the girl who died in front of her. The idea haunts her that she might have stopped it. Saving Julia is that thing for her, the thing that will help her put it behind… even if she's still uncertain about her dragon skills and has to go back to a place where she was tortured. That's my soul mate—willing to leap with her whole heart, even when she's not at all sure she's ready. That's literally how I'm standing here a mated dragon today… and I couldn't love her any more for it. Plus there's the practical matter that Cinder's the only one who can take us to Julia because she's the only one who knows anything about her.

"All right, let's link up." Niko joins hands with Ember, who clasps hands with Cinder. I've already got my arm around her waist, so I offer my other hand to Constantine. "Cinder, you've got the lead," Niko says once we're linked. "Find Julia for us, so we can bring her home."

My mate nods and closes her eyes.

Teleportation is fucking strange. I'm still not used to it. And it's a bit nauseating when the shift is big enough. But one moment we're all standing in a short line in the meeting room, linked together… the next, we're in a workshop of some kind with workbenches and shelves and crap everywhere. There are potions and bottles and books—lots of ancient books—but what instantly captures everyone's attention are three people in the room. One is a rail-thin dark-haired girl who looks bad—like emaciated-and-tortured bad. The other is the red-haired witch, Alice. And the third… is a fucking Vardigah.

Everyone springs into action, but there are too many of us and not enough space. The room is narrow, and a table filled with potions blocks the center, plus the three of them are at the far end. The girl—it has to be Julia—is bound to a wooden chair, just an ordinary one, not like the torture chair we found Cinder in. But her hands are tied with rope to the arms. The witch is on one side, dressed in a long-sleeved, hooded cape, only with the hood down and her long red hair everywhere. She has her palm on Julia's head, but she's as shocked as the other two as we rush toward them. The Vardigah lets out a roar and gets off a blast of energy that hits the table and throws it back into the five of us. I step in front of Constantine—he's the only one without super strength—and use my new mated strength to block the table from taking him down. There's glass everywhere as bottles shatter. Ember gets knocked to the ground by something flying off the table, but Cinder's already helping her up. Niko is *gone*. Over the upturned table, now lying on its side, I see him at the far end, wrestling with the Vardigah.

"Fuck!" Teleportation. Of course. I will myself to the fight, slamming into the Vardigah when I arrive to throw him off balance. Niko goes down with him.

"My helmet, Aleks!" Niko screams in my ear.

What the fuck? Oh. Shit. Niko's going to *bite* the asshole, and he can't do that with his helmet on, and he can't get it off while wrestling with the Vardigah.

Ember and Cinder appear by the two women—Julia and the witch. The witch steps back, hands raised, but she looks mostly surprised, not like she will attack. Julia's freaking out, tearing at her restraints. Ember and Cinder are working that problem. Constantine's still climbing over the table. I lunge forward and snatch Niko's helmet off. I'm afraid I nearly took his head off too, but he recovers, and with the Vardigah still pinned, Niko shifts. I'm knocked back because Niko's dragon is ten times the size and has suddenly taken up the entire room. The Vardigah screams, but it's cut off by the fact that his head is now rolling across the floor.

Okay, then. Obviously not going the poison route.

Niko shifts back, but his fireproof suit is now

wrecked, and he's naked. Cinder and Ember have Julia free. The witch has backed all the way to the wall, probably getting as far from the dragon as possible.

I flip up my visor so Niko can hear me. "Get Julia out of here. Go with them, in case more Vardigah show up—*shit.*" Constantine is sprinting toward the witch, who's standing up straight and doing something with her hands that can *not* be good. "I got this!" I yell to Niko as I go after them. *"Constantine!"* I growl.

He reaches the witch before me, and I see his hand on his dagger, but the witch meets him with her arm outstretched, palm forward, and he just... *stops.* Maybe he'll actually talk to her first. Niko reaches the women—Ember, Cinder, and Julia— and the four teleport away. Relief gushes through me. Now I need to get my sorry ass home—and Constantine and the witch—without getting dead. Because being mated is fantastic except that if I die, Cinder dies, and that's just not acceptable.

I turn back to see Constantine's visor is up and the witch's palm his planted on his forehead. She's tall like he is, so she can easily reach, but *what the fuck?* I dash toward him, planning to knock him away from whatever hold she's got over him—he's fucking standing there, letting her do this, and that's not right—but just as I get there, he whirls around and says, *"No!"*

I stumble to a stop.

He grabs my shoulders, eyes wide. *"Aleks,"* he breathes in a weird gaspy kind of way. "There are *more* of them. Dozens."

What the hell kind of hex has this witch thrown on him—

She comes up behind him. "Take this. And go. *Quickly."* Her accent is strange—thick—I think maybe Irish? And she's shoving some kind of black mirror in Constantine's hands—it's trimmed in ornate gold, but the center is solid black.

"What the hell?" I say.

Constantine takes the mirror, gives the witch another wide-eyed look, then turns to me. "Takes us home, Aleks. *Now."*

"What about *her?"* I throw my hands out in exasperation.

"She has to stay. To help free the others." I don't like the glassy look in his eyes. It's a hex, I'm sure of it—

But then his words register in my brain. "Wait, what others?"

"Soul mates." And now I understand the

amazement in his eyes. Because if Julia is alive, then it's possible she *wasn't* Yiannis's soul mate. And if there are others—what the fuck did he say? *Dozens.* They could save us—they could save the entire lair. But we can't rescue them now—I just don't have the capacity. We'll have to come back.

I lock arms with Constantine and teleport us home.

TEN

Cinder

DIRECTOR OF PHOTOGRAPHY Cinder Dubois

I thought seeing my name scroll on the credits of Ember's documentary—*our* documentary—about underage trafficking would trigger all the guilt one more time. Instead, I'm super proud of her and the project. It's kind of amazing to be in this mental space. *Happy.* A crazy new normal.

"It's really good," I gush quietly as I hug my sister. We're hanging out at the back of the small room we've cleared for the screening. It's in the dormitory Niko and his dragons have set up for all the trafficking victims they've rescued along the way. There's actually a strange assortment of women here, not just victims—some of the women are working their way through the lair or have wandered into the world of the dragons one way or another and have decided to stay. If a woman falls in love with a dragon who's not her soul mate—which to be honest is ridiculously easy to do—the couple usually moves out of the lair to set up a life somewhere else. They pretend they're not dragons and have normal lives... until the end. If the woman dies first, which is typical since we humans don't live as long, the sad shell of a dragon returns to the lair and his brothers gladly welcome him back. If it's the dragon—if the withering starts—they still come back and spend their final days here. It guts me that that's their fate, and I'm keenly aware of how close Aleks came to being one of them. He's downstairs now, visiting one of his friends in the hospice ward.

"You okay?" Ember asks, peering at me. I know she was worried the documentary might be triggering.

"I'm good. Great, actually." I smile at the women and girls filing out from the screening. One of them's pushing Julia in a wheelchair. Ember gives me a nod to go ahead, so I step up before they can escape from the room. "Hey," I say, kneeling next to Julia's chair. "How're you doing today?" It's only been a day, and she had much worse abuse for much longer than I did. It's going to take some time for her to recover.

"Hey, you." She smiles, but the hollows of her cheeks make me sick inside—the Vardigah basically starved her the whole time. "I'm doing good."

"You don't have to put on a brave face for me." I give her a gentle nudge. "I *know* how much it sucks."

"I know you do." Her smile dims a little, and she takes my hand to squeeze it. "I'll catch you later, okay?" Poor thing looks exhausted. I'm surprised she even made it out for the screening.

"You bet." I stand up to let her go. They're keeping her in the dormitory, but nearly every dragon in the lair is lined up, waiting for a chance to care for her. Niko decided rotations would be good—not run the risk like he did with Aleks. We were lucky I ended up his soul mate, but it could have been so much worse. Much more heartbreak. And no one needs that.

But I'll have to visit later and bring Julia some ice cream or something. Teleportation fucking *rocks*. There is no craving that has to go unsatisfied when you can bebop down in an instant to get some Chunky Monkey from Ben&Jerry's. I will gain a hundred pounds if I keep indulging in that, but I blame Aleks—he keeps wanting to show off his tele-portation skills. And we have legit reasons to prac-tice. I need to get good at my new dragon skills so I can help out when we go back to the Vardigah realm. Except somehow all our practice winds up with us teleporting back to the cottage and making out in the garden. Or fucking on the swing. Or experimenting with some new spot for me to worship at the altar of Aleks's cock.

In other words: *my life is amazing.*

Ember comes up behind me. "Did you really think it was okay?" She's talking about the docu-mentary now—I have to pull my head out of the love-cloud that I seem perpetually in thanks to my uber-hot dragon mate.

I turn and give her another hug. "Yes. When does it start screening for real?"

"I'm working on the distribution agreements now." Her eyes light up, and I know how important work is to my sister, so I'm glad. "Niko has a ton of contacts. We'll be definitely getting it out to festivals, online, maybe a streaming deal. And he has some contacts in law enforcement, too—we might get some showings at police departments around the country."

"That's fantastic. Let me know if there's

anything I can do."

"It's all good." She beams. "You have enough to keep you busy right now."

I don't know if she means hot sex with Aleks or learning dragon skills—probably both. "Speaking of things that keep me busy... I'm going to check in with Aleks and see how he's doing."

Ember waggles her eyebrows at me.

"Shut up." It's not like she's not banging her hot dragon day and night, too. At least, I assume. No news yet on the baby-making, but I'm sure it's not for lack of trying. Aleks is sure bent on it, and I can't bring myself to complain.

I shoo her away with my hands then turn to follow the last of the screening crowd out. The elevator takes me down to the hospice, which is an entirely different vibe. Lights are lower. There's a hush in the air and the vague scent of bleach. Which is funny since dragons don't get viruses or infections—their bodies simply shut down if they live too long without a mate. And being a mated dragon now, I can understand—I'm *alive* now in a way I never was before. Alive. Whole. And wildly, madly in love.

I peek into the hospice rooms until I find the object of that love. Aleks is in the second room with a dragon who looks like he has terminal cancer. *Terminal broken spirit* is the real cause. I pause at the door and pull out my new, compact mirrorless camera. Fits in my pocket but has a lot of the capacity of the one Aleks brought me that first time at the cottage, when I flirted with him and started falling head-over-heels in love. The camera is quiet, so I can snap a few pictures of Aleks and his friend —Grigore—without them noticing. As I do, it strikes me, the contrast between the unreal beauty of the man I love and the elegant, dying face of his friend. A man who looked much like my mate not long ago. They seem like they're almost done, so I don't intrude—but I make a mental note to come back and ask Grigore to share his story. I've been drawn more and more to my camera, and I suddenly know what my next project will be: documenting the lives and hearts of the dragons who are withering. It might be too late for them, even if we do, as Constantine promises, actually rescue all the soul mates the Vardigah have supposedly kidnapped. He says the witch, Alice, will help us… but we have to prepare. And wait for her instructions. It seems like a half-cracked plan, but I've seen worse. I've *done* worse, so who am I to judge? But right here, right now, *these* dragons are dying. And I want to capture the amazing beauty of their lives before they pass.

I don't have to wait long before Aleks emerges from the room.

"Hey," he says. "I didn't know you were out here."

"Just seeing if there's some hunky dragon who'd like to have some wild sex. I hear dragons are into that sort of thing."

He smirks and slides his arms around me, holding me smashed up against his chest. I love the feel of him—always—but especially when he gets just a little riled up and possessive.

"You know," he says, "all other men will disgust you now."

"Is that right?" I mean, he's not wrong, but—

"Yes." He pulls me in to nip at my ear. "That's part of the deal. The mating. It means only my cock will satisfy you."

And *oh* does his cock satisfy. "I don't know." I squirm a little away. "That Niko is pretty hot. Maybe he's into threesomes with twins—"

Aleks growls and holds me tighter. "That's not funny."

"It's *hilarious.*" I wiggle until I get my hands free enough to run them up into Aleks's hair, making it a sexy mess. "Have you met Niko? He's as wild as a crosswalk."

He scowls. "You don't know him like I do."

I draw back, feigning shock. "How well *do* you know him?"

"All right, enough of you, Missy." He reaches down and hoists me over his fucking shoulder!

I almost shriek—I have to clamp my hand over my mouth, so I don't disturb everyone in the ward. *"What* are you doing?" I hiss. My ass is way up in the air.

He swats my bottom. "There's a certain dungeon I've been meaning to introduce you to—a place where naughty little girls get their just desserts for their sassiness."

"Are you kidding me?"

"Not even a little." He squeezes my ass, and before I can blink, he's teleported us to what looks like a dominatrix's playroom. All kinds of restraints and harnesses, and I swear I see something like a swing...

"Holy... *fuck,*" I breathe.

"Oh yeah." His voice is rough. "We're going to be here for a while."

And if there's one thing I know about the dragon I love—he always keeps his promises.

Cinder and Aleks have their HEA, but Constantine is determined to rescue the rest of the captured soul mates. Will he find his own? Find out in *My Dragon Mate* (Broken Souls 3).

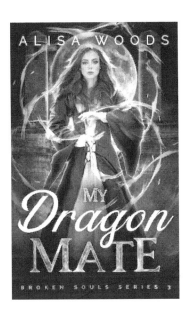

Get My Dragon Mate today!

Subscribe to Alisa's newsletter

for new releases and giveaways

http://smarturl.it/AWsubscribeBARDS

About the Author

Alisa Woods lives in the Midwest with her husband and family, but her heart will always belong to the beaches and mountains where she grew up. She writes sexy paranormal romances about complicated men and the strong women who love them. Her books explore the struggles we all have, where we resist—and succumb to—our most tempting vices as well as our greatest desires. No matter the challenge, Alisa firmly believes that hearts can mend and love will triumph over all.

www.AlisaWoodsAuthor.com

Printed in Poland
by Amazon Fulfillment
Poland Sp. z o.o., Wrocław

49934640R00101